I

The Scratchers

By Charles Hammer

Cover design and photo illustration by Elise Ray,
eliseray.com

Free Kansas Publishing
4829 Black Swan circle
Shawnee KS 66216
Hammerc12@gmail.com
Copyright 2013
ISBN-13: 978-0615849331
ISBN-10: 0615849334

The Discovery

The river came out of the hill. Its black water welled in a sun-dappled pool, then tumbled down and away over stones of the rapids below. The cavern from which it flowed breathed a welcome coolness on the faces of three boys who labored there. They tightened the last wires binding together a boat they had built of wooden crates and empty gasoline tins. Then they stared nervously back into the cave, into a darkness they hoped to make light.

It was July 20, 1912. That morning Count Henri Begouen had waved goodbye to his three sons as they left the manor house on what he surely took to be a fool's errand. It seemed that his sons, Max, Jacques and Louis, had been caught up in the fever of discovery then sweeping through their beloved French Pyrenees mountains.

Only 33 years earlier, the first of the Stone Age art caves had been discovered at Altamira, Spain, not 300 miles to the west. It was immediately declared a fraud. Hadn't Bishop Ussher of Armagh calculated from the generations listed in the Bible that the world was created in 4004 B.C.? How, then, could people have made a great cave art which began 30,000 years ago and died away 20,000 years later? Blasphemy!

But discoveries of art caves continued, swept eastward into France. For years the fireside of Count Begouen's estate of Montesquieu-Avante had been haunted by tales of nearby cave art finds. Which is why the three brothers were now wading and paddling up the Volp river into the cavern.

The stream was at its summer low. Still, they had to lie flat on the boat, hands groping along the overhead rock to drag themselves upstream. Daylight dimmed behind them as darkness grew ahead. They lighted lamps, which after long minutes revealed a rising arch of stone above. The tinny clanking of gas cans echoed in an underground chamber with a gravel beach, where they disembarked.

Scattered amid the gravel were broken flint points, fragments of bone and antler worked by humans. Probing down a short passage, the boys stepped into another room—stunned at the blaze of light shining back from crystal walls and stalactites. On the walls they saw engravings of animals. Amazed, delighted, they reversed course and hurried home to tell their parents what they had found.

Five months after three brothers discovered the art cave in 1912, Begouen family members and archaeologists posed with their exploration boat where the Volp river emerges from the cavern. Left to right they are Jacques Begouen, his father, Count Henri Begouen, Max Begouen, the archaeologist Henri Breuil, Louis Begouen, and archaeologist Emile Cartailhac.

On October 12 of that same year, Max and Louis and a friend, Francois Camel, re-entered the cavern and struggled back to a point where the passage was blocked by a stalactite curtain. They broke through and penetrated more than 1,500 yards into the hill, where they found bisons sculptured in clay.   This river cave they named for a nearby locale, Tuc d'Audobert.

Two years later, on the other side of the same hill, the three brothers lowered themselves on ropes through a hole in the earth to discover a second cave, which overlapped the first but did not connect. For obvious reasons, this cave was named Trois Freres—Three Brothers. The Abbe Henri Breuil, foremost cave art expert of the early 20th Century, judged that until some old collapse of rock closed the passage, the two caves had been joined.   Abbe Breuil concluded that the engravings on the cave walls were created about 15,000 years ago

While many of them are now famous, one of the most obscure is even more intriguing. On hard limestone the artist scratched what seems to be a boy's face, smiling so strongly that his eyes squeeze nearly shut. It is the only fully human face that looks out from the walls of Trois Freres.   Crude and quickly drawn, it is much in the style of far more expert engravings found a hundred miles north in a rock shelter called La Marche.

The overhang in La Marche cliff looks out over a lush valley and small stream.   Far longer than anyone today remembers, humans had used it—most recently as a barn.   In 1937 Leon Pericard, an army veteran wounded in World War I, saw a picture scratched on a limestone plaque he lifted from the shelter's dust.

He dug and found more. Wisely, he called in archaeologists, first the Abbe Breuil, much later Leon Pales and Marie Tassin de Saint-Pereuse, who at last deciphered the tablets' confused tracery of lines, picture on top of picture created possibly by several artists over many years. Those artists show we modern people how our ancestors of the Old Stone Age looked—how they wore their hair, cut their whiskers or left them long, how they belted their garments and perched hats on their heads. Archaeologist Evan Hadingham wrote that Pales with help from Saint-Pereuse had revealed an Ice Age portrait gallery.

"These together constitute well over a quarter of all the human figures known in Paleolithic art," he said. "La Marche stands at least one traditional assumption on its head—namely, the proverbial reluctance to depict the human form. Then the faces themselves contrast remarkably with the animalized profile so familiar from other sites. The La Marche heads are unquestionably human."

Paleolithic artists created their work over a period of more than 20,000 years—two hundred centuries. Of all the human images ever discovered from that era, more than one-fourth were found in this dusty hillside hole 20 yards deep, 20 yards wide. And these the most truly human of all.

It's often said that there's nothing new under the sun, today perhaps with good reason. But there was a time when new things happened, when people first discovered they could express their thoughts and feelings through art, as the actual cave images accompanying the text of this novel prove.

What happened at La Marche so long ago? What happened at Trois Freres? How was this art made? What on earth happened?

1

Air

The river came out of the hill, came right out of a hole in the hill. Black water poured out, shading to blue as it swirled into a pool just below.   Then it roared down and away, foaming over the stones of a rapid.

Staring back into the darkness, Nyori could see space between the river and the arch of rock above. The hole exhaled the musk of old earth, cool on the skin of her arms. It might be a cave.   She had lived most of her life in or near caves yet had never seen the pictures deep inside their summer home, Owl Cave. Her own people forbade it.   Would there be pictures in this river cave, where nobody lived? Nyori wondered.

The two boys ran around the sloping shore of the pool toward the dark opening. Soon they came back, walking in the water. They were spoiling their leather sandals, which would shrink and twist in drying.

"Water cold!" Otti shouted.

Otti was her brother.   He'd lived through only eight winters, five fewer than Nyori, who was almost a woman. Anzeel was a friend, older than she but still not smart enough to keep his sandals dry.

"It could be a cave," Anzeel said, "but we can't go in. Far back inside, rock comes right down to the water."

"I dive under rock, I swim under," Otti said. "I come up inside, inside cave Me!"

"Go ahead," Anzeel told him.

"There may be no coming up," Nyori said, "may be water all the way. No air."

She sighed and gestured toward the horse colt, stretched limply out where it had finally collapsed on the bank of the pool. They had work to do. Nyori took a flint knife from the pouch at her waist and knelt beside it. Grasping the tawny softness of its pelt at the dewlap, she lay the chipped edge against the warm flesh. Nyori was of the Horse Band, yet she did not believe in Irta, nor in the other gods that her band's Scratcher preached. Still, she bowed her head now and closed her eyes.

"I'm sorry, little colt."

Then she opened her eyes to slice straight down the animal's belly. The flint cut through hide and then white fat deeply enough to make blood ooze. She cut again, trying to get through the muscular body wall without piercing the guts, which would smell awful. She wanted the guts out to lighten the carcass so they could drag at least one haunch of it back to Owl Cave on the other side of the hill. Nyori also wanted the liver. She was hungry. They could eat the liver raw or even cooked, since she carried firestone and a fire flint in her pouch.

They had driven the colt out of a herd in a fern meadow down the hill. Nyori hit her once with a lance, but poorly. Anzeel's lance struck deep into the chest. He was a strong thrower. By then the animal was running madly. In full run, even badly hurt, horses go far. Not that the grown-ups back at Owl Cave expected children to bring home meat, but they would be pleased with this fat carcass.

"I dive under rock," Otti said again. "Come up again. Air. Be air inside."

Something was wrong with Otti, his sister had known it for a long time. He was dumb, a sweet boy but really dumb—not like Anzeel, who was just maddeningly careless about certain things. Her brother learned so slowly.

"I dive under rock," Otti said, "I can."

"Go ahead," the older boy said. "I dare you."

Nyori's rage boiled up. Otti didn't understand danger. He might really try it.

"Anzeel!" she shouted. "Leave him alone!" She blazed at him with her eyes, the boy throwing up his hands as if to shield himself from their glance, deadlier than fish-spear barbs. He laughed and staggered backward. Nyori stiffened her lips so she wouldn't smile at his craziness. "Anzeel, help me butcher! We can roast the liver and eat before we walk home."

But he turned away from her and stared again into the dark hole where the river came out.

"Maybe Otti's right," he said. "What if there *is* a cave that goes through the hill to Owl Cave on the other side. Scratcher took me way deep in Owl Cave. I could find my way through Owl Cave. Maybe I could go in here, then right on through to get home quickly."

Because Scratcher was going blind, the Horse Band needed someone to replace him. The old man had taken Anzeel far into the cave and taught *him* how to make pictures. Scratcher refused to let Nyori go along, even to watch, because that would anger Irta, god of Deep Earth. So proud for himself was Anzeel that he had not helped Nyori argue her case. The angry burning started again in her belly. For as long as Nyori could remember, she'd been scratching practice pictures into dirt, onto stone or bone, on the wide shoulder blades of reindeer, even a few pictures on entrance walls of caves. But they never let her see Deep Earth pictures. That no woman was allowed to do, and certainly no girl..

Ever since she could remember, they had said she shouldn't or couldn't. Lee-tan was the worst, a lazy woman who never even *wanted* to do anything different, so she said no girl should do it either. Nyori felt hungry and tired and weary even of herself—that she no longer seemed bound to anyone, not even to women of the Horse Band who had mothered her. She caught herself muttering, "Can't! Can't! Can't!" Sawing the chipped edge violently back and forth through the animal's flesh. She stood up and turned away from the boys, groping blindly with her fingers to stuff the bloody blade back into the pouch. Instantly, Anzeel turned toward her and tried to look serious.

"All right, Nyori, I'll butcher. Don't get mad."

She stood on the slope and looked out over the Land, seeing first the cave hill rising on her left. Beyond it rose more hills slanting up in ranks toward peaks of the Blue Mountains, sunlight gleaming on their glaciers, the sky a brilliant blue between white cloud towers. To her right the earth tilted down, then rose up again to a lower hill and turned down once more, hill after hill rolling away endlessly toward the Cold Sky, where—a whole moons' walk away—the Great Ice covered all.

Yet here the hills were darkly green, spring arriving early. Soon the horse, the roe deer and red deer, the bison and antelope, even a few shambling mammoth with their stained ivory tusks, would graze these valleys upward toward the mountains. The Horse Band always came before them, making ready for the best hunting of the year. Nyori liked the season, liked to look out now over meadows spotted with the five-petaled white of thorn-rose. Her angry panting had given way to long smooth breaths.

But, turning back, she saw Anzeel after all had not stooped to butcher the horse. Now he danced backward away from Otti, who tugged and jerked at his leather tunic, trying to hold the older boy. Scuffling together on the bank of the pool, the boys giggled and slumped weakly against one another. This time it was Otti, her own brother, who provoked it.

"I dare *you*. I dare you dive under rock."

"I said it first," Anzeel laughed. "I dared first. *You* dive under the rock. *You* swim through the hill."

Nyori watched their baby-play, feeling inside the sudden weight of her years. Few of the Horse Band lived through thirty winters. Nyori's own mother had been killed after only twenty. I myself may die soon, Nyori thought, sooner, younger than my mother. And she had not even seen the Deep Earth pictures, certainly had no chance to make one. They would never give her a chance.

"No, you dive, you!" Otti shouted. They pushed and pulled one another, giggling, staggering from side to side.

The burning in her belly now rose with the flush of hot blood through her face. She felt the wetness of water on her ankles but had walked far into the pool before the cold, as of melting ice, began to numb her sandaled feet. She held her arms out for balance and stumbled anyway on the rolling gravel of the bottom. She splashed toward the opening where the stream came out, wading to thigh depth before the boys even noticed.

"Hey, don't. Nyori, don't!" She heard Anzeel's call but didn't turn. "I'll butcher the colt, Nyori. I will."

"What sister do?" Otti whined. "What she do-o-o-o-o?"

"I don't know. Nyori, come back! Don't be mad."

4

The lowering sun warmed her left cheek. With eyelids nearly closed, she glanced through blurry lashes and saw it, flaming in a sky more deeply blue than the pool around her. Then the overhead shelving rock of the cave mouth blocked its light. Again the earth breathed its musk on her face and chest. Compared to the ice that enwrapped her lower body, its breath now seemed steamy. She struggled waist deep through water like thick gruel that dragged against her leather trousers, the blue of it shading to gray and then black. From far behind came Anzeel's yell.

"Nyori, you stop! *STOP* it!"

They yelled and yelled. She had to shut them out. She had to focus on the cave ceiling as it descended stage by stage, until, with her mouth in water, the stone above scraped her skull. Whatever her other weaknesses, Nyori could swim. She knew the tricks. To keep nose and mouth above the surface, she rolled to her back and floated, kicking strongly against the current. She panted, panted, till dizziness fogged her brain—no longer panting in anger but to fill herself full, to charge herself with life. Her mouth, eager for air, sucked in bitter moss from the rock. She spat it out, took one more great breath and held it, then rolled belly down and kicked off.

Eyes open to the cold, she saw that the water, which had seemed so black, was quite clear. Light shone through it from behind her, shone under her, even reached a little ahead. She swam. She reached arms forward and flapped them back through melted ice as the white stork flaps through air.

Here the passage was so deep that the current slowed. Boulders on the stream bed glided swiftly beneath her, everything darkening as she swam onward, everything fading in her eyes as she burrowed toward the heart of Irta. Her right hand scraped stones at the side. She couldn't see the cave wall there. She swam upward, what she thought was up, but only bashed her head against the rock without finding air. Turned down again and swam on, weakening. Her chest did not hurt, it did not burn. It heaved, sucking inwardly at her mouth and nose. It wanted air, which only nose or mouth could give it. Her chest heaved, sucking, but she dare not open.

I could dive under rock. Be air. *AIR.*

Her eyes still open to the blackness, she saw herself then as from a distance, a drowned body, its skin tanned dark as the leather tunic it wore, floating backwards down the stream, emerging in sunset light to be found by Otti and a grief-stricken Anzeel, who, too late, would shed tears and be sorry, would regret the way he had treated his good friend, Nyori. That he had not helped her go to Deep Earth. Wherever I come out—if I come out—that will be a different world, she thought, and I a different person.

Her chest heaved, at last willing to open itself even to water, though she did seem to hear a splashing, as if far away this stream had a surface where water met the air.

2

A Different Person

Her head banged rock again and her hungry mouth turned up, this time finding air—now more than that finger's width. She spat water and sucked in sweet, shuddering gasps of it. She hung there, bracing herself in the angle between rock overhead and rock to the side. Current tugged at her legs, dragged at the sandals on her feet. She breathed and breathed, trembling with cold.

Her hand searched the ceiling, felt the rock slope gradually farther above the water. She thrashed in that direction through a darkness like death. She closed her eyes and saw flashes of light behind the lids, red animal shapes, but—afraid to blind herself this way—opened them again into deeper blindness. Her jaw trembled, teeth rattling in her head. As she paddled forward, the ceiling rose until she could no longer touch it. Then she found the pebbly bottom with her feet, and it rose, too, Nyori at last crawling out on what felt like a gravel beach, river on the left, smooth wall on the right.

She sat on the gravel with her back against rock, resting on a pile of dry sticks and twigs washed in long ago by the stream. She hugged herself as water drained from her tunic. The air felt warm against her skin. Her fingers squeezed the flesh of her shoulder, fingers like glacier ice, the shoulder glowing warm under them—not that it was really warm. Her lips drew back from her teeth in a grin of pain. Diving under the rock had made her a different person all right, a frozen person, exhausted and even hungrier. She heard the stream as it tinkled over tiny stones at the edge of the beach. Even fainter, because so far away, came the roar of a waterfall.

"Haaa-loooo!" she yelled, and got back her own voice, "Haaal-ooo...oooo..."

Blackness pressed against her face. She listened keenly, knowing that only this way could she detect the approach of danger. Long ago she had seen Scratcher mangled, nearly dead, after he fought the cave bear. It was Nyori's own mother, Anupa, who finally killed the weakened beast, stabbing straight to the heart with her lance. She shouldn't, they said, she couldn't—but she did, *she* killed it. Horribly mangled, Scratcher lived. Anupa, bitten only once, watched her leg turn black and then died, lay down and died of a wound Scratcher couldn't cure. He wanted to cure her, but Scratcher couldn't cure anything.

Here in the blackness, Nyori could not forget that bear, a heap of bloody fur big as ten Horse People, many times pierced, with a hot mouth that could enclose her whole head. She rubbed herself, felt the coarse scrape of callouses over her skin. She felt alive again, had started to wonder what next, when the water exploded with splashing and animal grunts:

"Wah! Wah! Ahhhhhhh!"

The bear came alive in her mind, she felt his breath in that grunting. She jumped up and banged against the cave wall, trying to escape. With one hand on the stone to guide her, she fled down the beach, tearing her sodden sandals, bloodying her feet on sticks and logs she couldn't see.

"Ahhhhhhhh!" came the roaring. "Ooooh! Ahhhh."

When it died into silence, she froze in place, terrified that her own panting would lead the bear to her hiding place. She studied the darkness that hid the animal. Suddenly it roared again.

"NYORI!" The first answer coming only from far depths of the cave, "NYORI...eeee...eeee...eeee.."

Instantly, she was furious.

"Anzeel! You left Otti out there by himself!" He didn't answer, he was still gasping for air. "Anzeel, you squirrel, you spider! You can't leave Otti alone!"

He sucked in a huge breath. She could hear it. Then he yelled back:

"I didn't! I dragged Otti in. Come help."

"Oh, you spider! You cockroach!" Stumbling toward the sound, she splashed into the water. "Where are you?"

"Here. Help me. Take one arm."

Blindly she pushed forward, falling down and getting up, until she heard Anzeel's breath. Together, with her leading, they dragged the limp child out onto the beach.

"He's not breathing! Anzeel, if you drowned my brother..."

"He *is* breathing."

Sure enough, she heard the boy's faint breath. Otti coughed, the breath came stronger. He coughed again and vomited, water splashing on the pebbles of the beach.

"Why did you follow me!" It was more accusation than question. Still he answered.

"Because I thought you were dead! You mole! You dumb dirt-mole, drowning yourself!"

As echoes roared around them, Nyori winced, sucking her head down between shrugged shoulders. She found Anzeel's arm with her fingertips and followed the sodden sleeve of his tunic down to the hand, which she placed against the cave rock.

"Sit down against the wall."

They sat close hugging each other, Otti's small body shuddering between them, her own face cradled so close to Anzeel's that she could feel his warmth. I'm glad he followed, she thought, an invisible smile stretching the skin of her face. She was proud of his strength, that he could make that swim towing Otti along. As water drained out of her leather garment, it began to feel warmer than the air. Gradually their shivering stopped. They sat there so long she began to feel sleepy. Then Otti sucked in a long breath and sighed out suddenly from the blackness.

"I dive under rock," he said. "I did!"

Nyori and Anzeel laughed, and Otti laughed at their laughter, echoes ringing around them. They were warm enough now to separate, sitting side by side with their backs against the stone. They couldn't see each other, they couldn't see fingers they held before their eyes. Anzeel said:

"You still have the firestone?"

Suddenly agitated, she groped at her sodden pouch, terrified that she might have lost her mother's firestone. She was the only child of the Horse Band who possessed one. Ah! She felt it, she weighed in her fingers the squarish lump, heavier than the rounded flint that she also brought out. Touched by water, the firestone always stained orange as ocher, but that never diminished its power. Striking flint against flint, you could never make fire. But flint against firestone, yes.

"Here! In my hand."

"Can you dry it enough to strike a spark?"

She felt along the cave floor to a pile of twigs, raised a handful to her nose and sniffed. Juniper resin! She reached out again and found juniper needles. They lay near flowing water but were dust dry. Nyori scrubbed flint and firestone through the litter to blot the water off them. Then struck them together. One spark flew off. In its flare she saw Anzeel's face filled with sober interest, his eyes looking not quite at her, yet in their paleness strangely beautiful. That beauty faded into blackness. She struck the firestone again, and the vision hung for an instant in her brain: gray rock of the cave wall behind two boys, a beach where water lapped, heaps of tree branches along the wall. From the darker blackness that followed, Anzeel said:

"This must be Owl river. It goes under ground on the other side."

With her fingers, Nyori scraped a little pile of needles together. She struck a spark, which glanced away at the wrong angle, going dead on the clay floor—silly of her. She had made many fires this way. She struck again and again, raining sparks into the tinder. One spark clung to a juniper needle, its light glowing on a curling wisp of smoke. Nyori breathed on it. In a moment she sucked in the tang of hot resin as a flame licked up. Anzeel added handfuls of needles, then twigs and larger branches. Otti tilted his sandaled feet up to the warmth.

Firelight showed up the cave around them, wide and dark with black water running alongside their beach. Nyori saw the rock overhead was high. Here and there water glittered on the walls, shining as droplets oozed slowly down.

"Is this Owl Cave?"

"I don't know," Anzeel said. "I never saw this."

Nyori rose to her feet.

"I don't want to swim back out through the water. You said this might go right through the hill into Owl cave. Let's go home that way."

"Nyori, the people will worry. They'll think the Wolf-Kill band got us. We better swim out."

"Wolf-Kills haven't bothered us for years. You said yourself you could get home quick through the cave."

"But that's *Deep Earth*," he groaned. "You're not supposed to go there. Remember, Irta..."

"*This* is Deep Earth," she broke in. "I don't see Irta. Do you?"

Anzeel's wide eyes searched the rock above where they stood, searched the walls, then came back to meet Nyori's. He shrugged.

"All right."

She was surprised that he so easily gave in. She looked at his face, scratched on forehead and cheek where he'd banged it swimming in, with his freckled nose and a little smudge of hairs trying to grow on his upper lip. For all of her yelling, she liked the way he was always ready to try something new.

"But we must take fire," he said.

He searched among the driftwood for the most resinous branches of juniper, broke them into easy lengths, then knelt and began splitting one with his flint knife, splitting it many times so it would burn easily. Each twiggy torch was held together only by a solid handle near the base. Nyori helped him. They worked a long time, made a pile of these torches and lighted two from the fire.

Their lances lay outside the cave beside the little horse. They started out along the gravel beach armed only with torches, now their only defense if they met a bear or cave lion. But fire was strong against animals. Where the river again dove under rock, they fought waist deep across it and climbed a little cliff toward a black hole, like another cave within the cave. Going through, they came out in a low room where wet rock hung in folds from the ceiling like the ice-white folds of a hide tent in winter. In the flicker of their torches, crystal walls blazed around them. Water-dripping stone fangs pointed down from the ceiling, almost meeting other fangs that rose from the floor. The three of them might have been standing in the wet mouth of some huge man-eater.

"Teeth-that-grow—that's what Scratcher calls them," Anzeel said. "They get longer, but slowly."

11

"I see bison!" murmured an awe-stricken Otti.

Nyori saw it too, the figure of a bison scratched on the wall, its head lowered as if challenging another bull of the herd. Farther along the one wall, there were pictures of horses, even one mammoth, none of them painted. The stone here was gray, covered with a soot-dark skin. The figures had been cut into the rock, animal outlines showing nearly white against the dark cover. Anzeel stood looking up at them, mouth open, wide eyes gleaming in torch light.

"Ancients made these," he whispered. Why was he whispering? "I saw some like them far back in Owl Cave. Scratcher says they're magic. I was scared to scratch on the walls, even with him there. He made me scratch."

Nyori moved close to the mammoth, which looked as if it had always been there in the rock, only waiting to be discovered. The Ancient had just scratched a few lines, placing them so that the mammoth's shoulder and hip bulged with muscle just where the rock bulged. She liked the sleepy line of the animal's eye, the dome of head curving down to a huge neck, a line of backbone arching on from there.

In the green world outside, the mammoth could chase a hunter down, yank him from the tree where he hid or uproot the tree and trample the man. Yet some Ancient had seized this mammoth and put it on the wall, even made the huge beast sleepy so that Nyori wished she could pet its hairy hide.

Long ago Nyori's mother, Anupa, had been so impressed by Scratcher, the great Scratcher, that she tried to learn his skill. The old man taught her a little, and Anupa taught Nyori. She bound leather around the butt of the flint so its sharpness would not cut her daughter's fingers. With Nyori's hand holding the tool, Anupa's hand enclosing hers, the flint point slowly made a noble red deer show itself on the bleached surface of a bone—the child's eyes widening in amazement.

"See, Nyori," her mother exulted. "It's *your* deer."

"Mine? Mi-i-i-i-ne?"

That astonishment still burned fresh in Nyori's mind. After that she scratched countless tiny red deer, reindeer, horses, the great bulls, even one sleek salmon, on bits of bone or stone or in the dirt of cave floors. But this in Deep Earth, this was big, this was powerful. It *was* magic to capture an animal that would live forever on the wall—just not

12

the magic Scratcher preached, what he called his Mysteries. Mysteries she could not believe, not since the cave bear killed her mother. Even now, standing before the mammoth on the river cave wall, she yearned to hear her mother's voice, feel that warm hand enclosing hers.

With her fingertips she felt a skin of water oozing down across the mammoth. Something in the water was covering the lines with a thinness like the outer dome of a reindeer's eye, except this was cloudy. Someday it would hide the picture. From her pouch she took a burin, a flint blade tipped with a pointed graver. She laid the point near the end of the mammoth's trunk.

"Don't!" Anzeel yelled. "It's forbidden to women!"

She started a new line just outside the old one, chips of the soft rock falling away under the hard flint edge. It left a sharp white path through the black.

"Oh, don't, don't!" Anzeel moaned.

He crouched below her, hands clutched over his head, as if he thought the cave would fall. Otti crouched beside him, whimpering.

"You're scaring my brother," Nyori told him.

In one smooth sweep of her blade, she drew upward along the outside line of the mammoth's trunk, over the forehead around the little head bump, down to the neck, 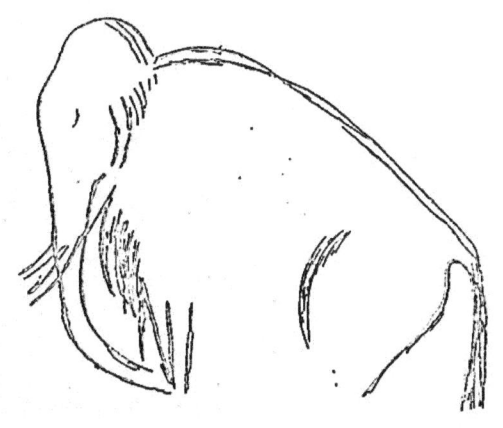 arching up again over the shoulders and down the long slope of back to the tail. With a few more strokes she slashed lines for the tusks, another little curve for the eye. She copied the original lines, that's all, renewing the shape so it would not be so soon covered by the cloudy film.

After awhile Anzeel rose to his feet, glancing uneasily into the dark spaces around them as if Ancients lurked there. He bent to Otti, urging the child to stand.

"All right," Anzeel breathed, "nothing happened."

He looked at the ground, then up at the mammoth picture, blinking in the glare of his own torch. He moved it so light fell edgewise on the wall. Running one finger along the line Nyori had cut, he brushed away clinging crumbs of stone.

"That's good," he said, and nothing more.

3

The Little Colt

As the first torches grew short, they lighted others from the dying flames. They crawled through narrow passages and picked their way across high spaces, whistling purse-lipped to hear the echoes. They scrambled upward through a hollow marrowbone of rock, Anzeel and Nyori helping each other. They reached down for Otti. He dangled from their hands, feet kicking, as they hauled him up.

The cave shrank inward so they had to crawl on their bellies, and they thought themselves stopped. Then it opened again into a smooth-floored chamber. She handed Otti her torch and dropped to her knees.

"Anzeel! Here's good clay! We could mold animals."

"Come on," he sighed.

She grubbed out a chunk of it and with fingertips crudely shaped a little bison statue.

"Try it, Anzeel!"

"No!" He dragged her onward. They soon arrived at another marrowbone, this one leading down. They wriggled through into a room below but, starting one direction, were blocked at the end. There, two big-eyed, round-faced owls stared out from the wall, their chick resting between them.

"Is this why they call it Owl Cave?"

"Maybe. Scratcher never took me here."

She held her torch low to make shadows in the deep-cut lines. The body of one owl looked more like a boulder than a bird. The baby owl's neck seemed broken.

"I can scratch a better owl," Nyori said.

Urging her on, Anzeel fretted that they would run out of branches and be trapped in the dark. After that they carried only one flaming torch, held vertically so it would burn slowly when they needed little light but turned down when they came to pictures so the flame would eat more wood and brighten. Otti jerked at her tunic, looking up at her, his tear-filled eyes full of torch light.

"Hungry!" he moaned.

She heard him but didn't hear him. She herself wasn't hungry anymore. She wandered on, looking up at the walls, filling herself full of pictures. She glimpsed part of a horse, high in a hidden corner and climbed a steep rock to see. It was a heavy-bellied mare, pregnant, marked with signs, each one a vertical line with a round shape protruding from it like the belly of a pregnant woman. Suddenly bold, Anzeel crawled up beside her and with his own flint knife scratched out another pregnancy sign.

"This makes many new colts," he said.

"I don't believe it."

"You don't believe anything."

"I don't believe his Mysteries, but I believe what Scratcher tells us to *do*," she said. "Many times he told us right. He saved us from the Wolf-Kills."

That story had been told and retold around Horse Band cook fires. When Scratcher was young, the Wolf Tribe—like the Horse Tribe—both were a part of the Steppe Peoples. Then in this far reach of the Land a conflict arose over dancing. Skuuhl, in those days young like Scratcher and chief of a Wolf Band, believed that to draw power from the earth, dancers should never lift their feet. They should shuffle along and stay in contact. Whereas others believed a lively hopping was the greatest tribute to Irta. It was the Shufflers against the Hoppers.

16

Scratcher didn't care. He would hop to please one side, shuffle to please the other. That worked well until one summer when Steppe People gathered for the Great River Conclave. There, while some shuffled and others hopped, the arguments grew heated. Suddenly Skuuhl swung his war club and bashed in the lead Hopper's head. Then all Shufflers drew out weapons and attacked those of Hopper belief.

Scratcher had foretold it and was ready. Among the whole Horse Tribe, he was first to lead his little Horse Band out, away into the night and, in following days, on into this lonely reach of the Blue Mountains. Scratcher had saved his band from the Wolves, who ever after had called themselves Wolf-Kills to frighten others. Because Scratcher saved them, that's why Nyori wished she could believe his Mysteries.

There was just one bad thing about *how* he saved them. Before that Conclave, lazy old Lee-Tan had been Skuuhl's woman. Then Skuuhl took other women to himself. Lee-Tan was furious. So when the Shufflers attacked, Lee-Tan fled with the Horse Band, bringing her nearly-grown son, Torfinn, with her. No longer the woman of a chief, she had lived in bitterness, striving to make a chief of her son and convert the Horse Band to Wolf ways. In recent days she'd been demanding that Torfinn—not Anzeel—take Scratcher's place. So now there were two ahead of Nyori—two! She would never, she thought, get her chance to be a Scratcher.

Pressing closer to the steep rock face, she saw the pregnant mare's head was held high, only one alert ear showing as if the other were hidden behind it. Or maybe this horse *had* only one ear. The head was just an outline—like the owls, as flat as the wall where it was scratched. The legs were different, inscribed so that the two on the far side showed behind the forward two, moving in a trot. This picture at least had some depth, but the line that curved from the animal's back around the haunch was all wrong. She reached toward it with her burin.

"Don't!" Anzeel shouted. "Don't touch it!"

"Everybody else changes pictures," she said. "You changed it." Nyori hated that word, *don't!* Her flint jerked out. Inside the thin line of the horse's back, she cut a thick new one, vibrating the point to wrap the mare in the shedding winter fur she would wear at foaling time in spring. Nyori arched the rump higher, tucked the haunch in further at the hamstring, then stepped back to study the effect.

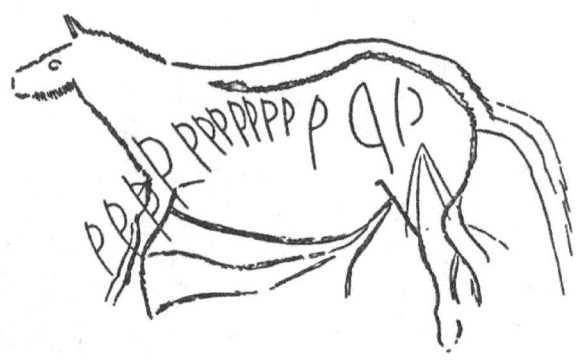

This time Anzeel refused to look. He wouldn't even look!

"You promise cook horse liver," Otti wailed. "Want liver!"

"Come on," Anzeel said, climbing down. "We have only three branches left to make torches."

She climbed down and lay a hand on Otti's damp hair, petting it, kneeling then to squeeze the child in one of her arms.

"We ate this morning. We won't starve."

With Anzeel leading, they moved on through dark passages, where, from holes in the floor, they heard the river roar far below. Once she heard sharp squeals, felt a leathery flapping around her ears. Bats! She ducked and covered her head and nothing happened. As they moved on, animals became thicker on the walls. She tried to keep Anzeel's torch for a guide in one corner of her eye as she lost herself in pictures. She saw a circle with human-like nose, eyes, and mouth—probably the Moon. That made her realize one thing was missing.

"Where are people?" she asked Anzeel.

"What?"

"No pictures of people here."

"We never scratch people."

"Why not?"

"It's dangerous. Make pictures of people, who knows what they do? Once I saw handprints on the wall. Nothing else of people."

Just then Otti stumbled over something. Long ago someone had carried in wood for a fire, which had burned itself out. It left this circle, nine inward-pointing branches with scorched ends.

"I remember this!" Anzeel cried. "We *are* in Owl Cave. From here I know the way."

Nyori and Anzeel knelt and began splitting the branches, their

18

hands blackening from the charred ends as they worked. Otti squatted to one side, tugged a small flint blade from his pouch and reached for a branch.

"I make," he said. "I too!"

She pushed the branch into his lap. With his dull blade, Otti gnawed at the wood while they finished the rest. With fire light assured, they started again, Nyori dragging behind the others, looking up at the walls.

Most animals of the Land had been trapped here, nearly all just scratched into the rock. Open eyed, Nyori saw how one by one they came into view, grew big in her vision, spreading themselves wide across the walls, then shrank and faded into darkness as she moved on. She felt dreamy, lost among the animals, until Anzeel jerked at her tunic. He tried to pull her quickly along the main path, avoiding the black mouth of a passage opening to the left. So! He didn't want her to go that way. Instantly, she shook free and turned into the passage.

"No, Nyori! That's the Womb Shrine!"

Womb Shrine—she'd heard the men call it Sacred of Deep Earth. Her torch shone on hanging folds of rock that rose higher as she moved. After hardly twenty steps, she came into a higher chamber, apparently a second route through this part of the cave. Why was it sacred? Then she saw the tracery of scratchings. Some animals were inscribed by themselves, others crowded together.

None of the early pictures had been marked out or damaged, but later scratchers had improved on old pictures or engraved new animals on top—bison, ibex, horse, reindeer, red deer, rhino, wild boar, cave bear and more. None was hidden, all were there, animals beside each other, on top of each other, some climbing straight up the walls, others hanging upside down, plunging and kicking, running and leaping, butting and bawling. In the dancing light of torches, the Womb Shrine pulsed with animal power, a great mixed herd like nothing in open air, like nothing else in their great Land.

Seeing it, she could almost believe this was the womb of Irta, a woman god who did not like women. Everything is born of Deep Earth. Only men go to the womb, not to violate but to plant these pictures like seed. Whatever they scratch on the walls, those things appear on the prairie above, on the tundra and the steppe, in the forest when animals drop their young.

"That's Scratcher's picture," Anzeel whispered.

It was another 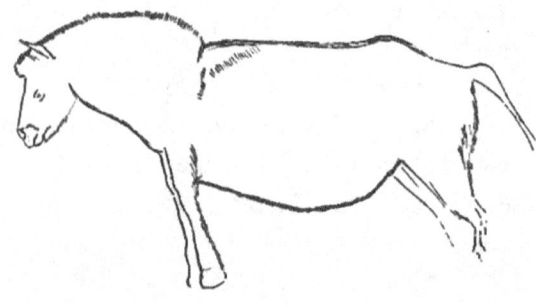 horse, a winter horse with heavy fur, probably a mare, though Scratcher had drawn in nothing except a big belly to show it. Heavy bodied, this mare, with powerful front legs but weak, back ones. Still, it was grand.

"This is Scratcher's?" she marveled. "How? He can hardly see."

"He made it last summer, before the blindness got bad." Anzeel's hand pulled at her. "Come *on*, Nyori! The people are worried. They'll be mad when they find out you went through Deep Earth."

She let him guide her down another passage swarming with animals. Without watching her feet, without watching the cave ahead—looking only at the pictures—she blindly followed. Only men could see Deep Earth, but here was Nyori, a girl who did not believe yet walked awe stricken through it. She shouldn't be here, of course she shouldn't. *Shouldn't!* Passing a bare place on the wall, she jerked free of him and groped for the burin in her pouch.

"Aw, Nyori..." Anzeel groaned.

"Hungry! Hungre-e-eee!" Otti cried..

Nyori now remembered the little horse colt in the fern meadow, the one they had killed today. Or was that by now yesterday? The colt had wandered away from its herd into trees, where the soil was moist. There ferns grew greener. She and Anzeel were downwind, yet as they moved up behind brush, the colt sensed them. Her head jerked up, her eyes widened.

Clinging to that memory, Nyori stepped up to the bare rock, struggling also to remember counsel given in past times by Scratcher and her mother: At the start always try to see the end. Look at the feet when you scratch the head. Draw loosely, don't dig in. Stand away from the rock, leave your body free to move.

She cut the outline in a few strokes, getting in both alert ears and all four legs, tensed for the run the little colt was about to make. Crumbs of stone fell away behind the burin's point. She drew the colt's small muzzle, her deep jaw, that wide and frightened eye. Nyori fought to create the animal as it stood tense in that single moment, but also to create the horse forever, in all its moments. That much she owed the colt whose life they had taken. She wanted her colt to be as good as, almost as good, as Scratcher's mare.

The shape complete, she cut the stone away outside, cut it on a slant so the horse would seem to stand out from the wall. That part took a long time. Finishing, she saw Anzeel and Otti had sat down to rest.

Sat right on the damp floor. Anzeel was holding his torch high, staring with his mouth a little open. He always let flies in when he was surprised.

"That's the horse colt we killed," he said.

Nyori knew it wasn't. No, this was a new thing she herself had made, the first big picture that was all her own. And it was also old— something taught to Nyori by her mother and Scratcher, taught to them by those who came before. Anzeel stood and moved closer, brushing dust from the seat of his tunic.

"That's good!" he breathed. "Better than I can do. With Scratcher going blind, it's better than he can do now."

Instantly, tears rose in her eyes, melting the scene before her, making it liquid and trembly. Her nose began to run. Snuffling, she wiped it with the back of one hand. For all his opposition, Anzeel was fair. She *liked* him. Nyori drew long breaths, struggling to calm herself. When Anzeel turned and saw her tears, his face grew tense with irritation.

"What's wrong *now*?" he said. He grabbed her hand and barked: "Come on!"

4

Home Again

Otti got so tired he asked to be carried. Anzeel took him first, carrying the child slumped across his back, sleepy head lolling forward over Anzeel's shoulder. They walked, hardly watching where they moved, no longer trying to find the way, only taking care not to turn on their own track. They walked.

She was so tired she didn't pause to look at pictures. Moving this slowly, they could not have come far through the cave, but it had taken a long time. Surely night had come and gone. It would be day again outside, or maybe night again. Anzeel tried to prove how strong he was. Nyori had to nag three times before, sighing, he took the torch and passed the baby over for her to carry.

Otti was a heavy baby, smelling of clay where his arms crossed in front of her neck, smelling of salt sweat despite his dips in water. Leaning to support the load, Nyori moved on, deciding she too would enjoy that—being carried again. When she was little and orphaned, all the women carried her.

She had been the darling of everyone, all except Lee-Tan and her son, Torfinn, who didn't like anybody because nobody else loved Irta as they did. Nobody else was so holy. Everyone else fell short. Nyori was exhausted now, carrying her sleeping brother as a real woman would, so sleepy herself she couldn't think. Anzeel touched her shoulder.

"Give him."

He handed her the burning torch and pulled Otti from her back, swinging the child around to his own. Now Nyori seemed to float up from the leather of her sandals. Otti's eyes came open, blinking.

"Home?"

"Almost," she told him.

It was true. Anzeel found more and more pictures he had seen before.

"Look! This one Scratcher did when he was teaching me."

He moved on as she raised her torch to the wall. It was a cave lion, the big cat's round ears raised to listen, its wide eyes staring into Nyori's own. She liked the round ears. She loved the light that glowed in those very different two eyes. Nyori couldn't make eyes like that.

But the body of the lion was a blob, or maybe two lion bodies stretching away in opposite directions from the head. Was this the best he could do now? She felt sad for him.

"Come on, Nyori! I can't see without the torch."

She caught up, beginning to think of the word Otti had used, "home." The best home she knew was the high space near the mouth of Owl cave, sun piercing the rock entrance to blaze on the dusty floor, two or three cook fires burning, the people chipping flint, carving bone or ivory, working leather as a couple of women nursed babies. An ordinary scene, that's how she saw it in her mind. But the sounds they began to hear ahead—chirping, keening, agonized sounds—were far from ordinary.

"Ay-yi! Ay-ye-ye-ye-ye! Ay-yi-yi-yi-yi!"

Anzeel's hand grabbed her upper arm, pulling her to a stop.

"Somebody died," he said.

"Who? Who died?"

"I don't know."

Torchlight showed her the soft hairs on Anzeel's upper lip,

which trembled now as he listened. Tears drew slow lines downward through the mud on his cheeks.

"Ay-ye-ye-ye-ye! O-wo-wo-wo-wo-wo!"

When he said her horse picture was good, Nyori herself had made tears. But she was surprised now that Anzeel could do the same. She wouldn't cry. No. She pressed one knuckle up beneath her nose to hold it back. Then, once again, her vision of Anzeel melted, trembled like his lip, dissolved in winking stars of torchlight.

Her Horse Band belonged to People of the Steppe, from the grasslands, the prairie that stretched away into the sunrise sky toward the End of the World. Ages ago, longer than anyone could remember, they had traveled toward the sunset to reach this blessed and various Land, a place which had tundra and prairie but also forest, valleys, hills and mountains too high to climb. The Horse Band was a fragment of the Steppe People, but they were not *of* them. As fingers and toes, ears and lips are part of one person, they were *of* their own little band, the Horse Band. And so was Nyori.

When she swam into the cave, she had thought she would escape, break free and become a new person in a different world. Now, hearing this agonized chanting of her people, she realized the long trip through the earth, among pictures by the Ancients, had only brought her home again. Still she felt new. She shook her arm free, took that hand of Anzeel's in her own and tugged him forward.

The passage opened out as they moved, ceiling rising higher. Walls smooth as horse-gut, shining with water, widened with every step they took. Now they heard not just the wailing but, even louder, angry voices of people arguing. Ahead they saw light, which brightened as they approached.

The last opening was low. This, she realized, was the Deep Earth Arch, through which Nyori had always yearned to pass—from the outside in. Now for the first time she would go through, but from inside out. She took a deep breath and sighed it away. They dropped their torches and bent to squeeze through, Nyori sheltering Otti's head with her hands to keep it from bumping.

Emerging, she stood up and sucked in a great breath. It was thick with smoke and the sweat-smell of her people, piercing and sweet to her as the breath of Spring. The children huddled together near the

25

cave wall, alongside the arguers, alongside the crowd of mourners.

"Ay-ye-ye-ye-ye-ye!"

Three great fires blazed in corners of the chamber, flickering on the ceiling, breathing a haze of smoke through the upper reaches of air. The sun's angle, slanting through the cave mouth, told her it was morning outside. Night had come and gone, but not even the morning of the second day. In the great room were gathered the Horse Band, nearly forty people dear to Nyori. They looked dirty and tired, as if they hadn't slept either—too wrung out with argument to notice three children. Drogben, a big hairy man, stood wild eyed before them, yelling at Scratcher.

"You coward! We got to fight the Wolf-Kill! They came back to the mountains and took ours. Now we fight!"

"They haven't come back," Scratcher said. "Anyhow, they're too many to fight."

Scratcher had lived many winters, a man so old his hair had thinned, bald skin gleaming through it in the firelight, so short that his weak eyes had to look up into Drogben's face. Scratcher's own face showed white scars from his long-ago fight with the bear. Drogben was younger but also scarred from battles with Horse Band enemies. He leaned close to shout at the old man.

"You don't care about ours then! You let us get murdered!"

Nyori was puzzled. Who had been murdered? Her eyes searched the Band and found no one missing.

"We can't beat Wolf-Kills in a fight," Scratcher yelled back. "I'll beat them with the Mysteries."

"Your *Mysteries*!" Drogben snorted. "HA!"

Nyori loved Scratcher, she loved Drogben. Hearing them scream at one another, she felt a stabbing in her heart.

The crowd stirred as Torfinn came through. His mother, Lee-Tan, pushed him from behind, propelled him forward, all the time talking into his ear—his holy mother, lazy old Lee-tan. Torfinn was older than Drogben, yet his skin was soft and pale. The only scars he bore had been carved into his face when he was a little boy and by his own mother, who said they made her son godly. Never strong in hunting or in battle, he stepped out now before the people. His mother fell on her knees, raising her arms to him.

"Praise Irta! She has sent us this sign. She took away Anzeel because she wants Torfinn to be our new Scratcher. Torfinn, the Holy Shuffler who draws power from the earth. Praise Irta! She wants Torfinn to lead us."

Nyori's breath came in sudden gasps. Took away *Anzeel*? Was it Anzeel who had been murdered, he and Nyori and her brother, Otti? They were supposed to be dead! She shrank back into shadows as a groan rose from the crowd. Torfinn was no scratcher. He couldn't make pictures. Yet Lee-Tan had been furious when she found out old Scratcher was preparing Anzeel for the job.

"Oh, praise to Irta," she shouted now. "Praise to this Shuffler man, Torfinn. He will save us from the Evil, save us from the false Scratcher."

The crowd groaned again, though two or three supported her with shouts of "Praise Irta!" Lee-Tan herself began to shuffle, keeping feet always on the ground, moving slowly through a little circle. Strangely, Scratcher then raised his face to the rock above, threw his arms wide.

"Praise Irta! Praise Her! Yes!" Scratcher shouted. "But not the Wolf-Kill Irta, who drinks human blood."

Amazingly, Scratcher—the great leader of the Hoppers—began to shuffle like Lee-Tan. Nyori's lips struggled against a smile. He would do anything to win out and keep the peace.

"Wolf-Kill Irta, the one true god!" Lee-Tan cried, still shuffling. "You of the Horse are fallen ones. Oh listen, oh listen to Irta's prophet!"

As if her words had cut tendons binding Torfinn's thoughts, his voice shrilled out.

"If Wolf-Kills took the children, Irta decreed it! Irta! Irta!" He too began to shuffle, turning circles wider than his mother's. "Wolf-Kills are the Sanctified, only they are earth-clingers, Shufflers who follow the good old ways!"

Old ways! Torfinn's words set Nyori to boiling. The Wolf-Kills couldn't make pictures. They knew nothing about the Ancients.

"Praise Her! Praise Irta!" Lee-Tan was urging now.

Nyori couldn't hold it in. This time she groaned when the crowd groaned, but Anzeel's hand clamped tight across her mouth. Scratcher had been a good leader. Following him, the Horse People had always escaped their enemies, always found enough to eat and good caves for shelter. For that reason few believed Lee-Tan's raving. Certainly not Drogben, who argued with Scratcher but always followed the course agreed on. Now the hairy man just stepped to the front, his brown bulk hiding Torfinn from view. As if nothing else had been said, he took up his dispute with Scratcher.

"We got to find the Wolf-Kills," he shouted. "Get the children back."

"We don't know Wolf-Kills took them," Scratcher said. "Maybe it was bear. Maybe cave lion."

"Cave lion? HA! There was no blood but horse blood, where they cut the dewlap. No, the children were butchering the colt, and the Wolf-Kills took them. You won't admit it, because you're scared to do anything—scared!"

"Can't *fight* Wolf-Kills," Scratcher said. "I can beat them with the Mysteries. I'll bring the children back."

"Ha!" Drogben yelled. "Ha!"

"*Mysterie-e-e-e-e-e-s!*" Scratcher sang out.

His bare feet stopped their shuffling and started hopping in a daring little dance. He threw his hands up in wild gesture, whirled them above his head. His stringy arms were wrinkled, his old elbows calloused as mammoth hide. His feet pounded the ground in drumbeat Hopper rhythm. The people watched, a few of them grinning, as he

wiggled fingers to suck down the spirits whirling in the air. Too many times the people had watched Scratcher try tricks that didn't work. The old man hopped and bounced and hopped again. Suddenly Nyori saw it: the picture of Scratcher that she would someday cut into rock—crude and rough, every deep wrinkle and crease showing. She didn't know how to draw people, had never seen a human pictured.   Still, in her mind she saw him.

Lee Tan couldn't bear looking at him, the old Hopper who had just defeated her once again.   Her burning eyes, snow-lynx eyes, roved darker regions of the cave as if looking for prey. They settled on Nyori, then on Anzeel, still bent under the burden of Otti. But these children who had vanished were prey the snow lynx couldn't quite swallow. Nyori saw Lee-Tan's eyes open wide, close and open wider.

"Yaaaaaaaa!" the woman screamed, backing away. She fell down, got up and fell again, scrambling to turn and flee back through the crowd.

Drogben was next to see them.   Red flames from the fire flashed in his eyes. He turned away and hurled himself through the crowd, as a boulder from an avalanche trap smashes through a herd of reindeer. People were flung aside. Then they were all up and running, scrambling for the far wall of the chamber, where they clustered to look fearfully back at these child-ghosts risen from the dead.

All except Scratcher, who never moved, an old Hopper standing alone now and rock solid on the earth as any Shuffler. He couldn't see well enough to be scared. Hands still raised, fingers still wiggling amid the spirits, he stared at the children with half-blind amazement. Then Nyori saw the old slyness shine through the murk of those eyes.

"It's the Mysteries!" Scratcher boomed in his loudest, deepest voice. "The Mysteries brought the children back!"

Amid rebounding echoes, Nyori reached a hand out, taking gentle hold of Anzeel's arm. She didn't turn to look at him. Barely moving her lips, she whispered:

"Anzeel, you are rigtht! It's the Mysteries, the Mysteries that brought us back."

5

Nothing bad happened!

The hugging went on for a long time. People swarmed about them, women first with their squeezes and pets, nuzzling their noses into Nyori's neck, stroking her hair.

What the melting ice of the river hadn't done, Nyori thought, the women were doing to Anzeel, who looked strangled in the arms of his Aunt Mayro and his mother, Kansi. Cheemee and the other women petted Otti, who smiled sleepily as he sat in the dirt. Even Riba petted him, Riba, who unlike Nyori was old enough to be called a woman now.

Some of the Horse People wept with relief, even some of the men, Wanchuck and Rothgar. They had so few, the Horse Band, and three had been lost, three of the most precious. Now they had come back. The men pushed in to hug them, each with his own particular odor of sour meat or sweat or leather—some better, some worse, but all smelling sweet as the thorn-rose now to Nyori. Drogben seized her shoulders in his great hands, hairy knuckled, and held her high, gently shaking as if she were red-meat salmon from the river. His face split in a white grin as tears ran down his cheeks.

The fires had burned low before they finished with the hugging. After that came questions. Nyori told how they had killed the little colt, how they swam into the cave and wandered dreamily past pictures scratched by the Ancients. From the back of the crowd came an angry roar.

"A girl saw pictures!" It was Torfinn, who paced angrily back and forth. "Deep Earth is sacred to men!"

This time he caught Scratcher by surprise.

"Why do you say that?" the old man asked.

"It's Irta's Law! Everyone knows!" Torfinn rumbled. *"Skuuhl* told us! *You* told us! *You* told us it goes against Irta. So you said!"

"He's right, Scratcher," Mayro broke in. "That's what you told us."

Of course she spoke the truth, but why would a woman—barred forever from Deep Earth—take Torfinn's side? Scratcher glanced about nervously, waving his hands as if once again he needed spirits of the air.

"Not every time. For instance, since Nyori was in Deep Earth, we've already had good luck. The Mysteries brought the children back."

"Yes, praise Irta!" cried Anzeel's mother.

A pleased murmur ran through the crowd. Instantly, Torfinn swung around on the children, rapping hard knuckles against Anzeel's chest.

"How *did* that happen? Anzeel, how *did* you come back?"

The boy glanced at Nyori, his eyes glinting in firelight, eyes of pale blue, more beautiful than the sky of dawn. Nyori stared back at him, stared deeply into those eyes.

"We were lost," Anzeel said, "lost bad, deep in the cave, and then we came out. Scratcher saved us."

She liked his answer—as much like the truth as a lie. Scratcher lowered his eyes to the earth, where his thick-nailed big toe was drawing circles in the dirt.

"It wasn't me," he sighed. "Mysteries did it."

That satisfied the people, but the happiness that came with the children's return had passed. Rubbing their eyes, yawning, they looked sleepy and irritable. Lee-Tan stared sourly at Nyori. She took Torfinn's oak staff and slashed it through the air.

"They didn't tell us where they were going," Lee-Tan said. "They scared us. For that they need whipping."

"Whip them!" Torfinn cried.

Sitting spread-legged in the dirt, Otti started wailing. He opened his mouth and bawled at the cave ceiling. Mayro knelt to comfort him.

"Not Otti."

"Then the other two."

Lee-Tan brandished the staff again.

"I whip them."

This didn't scare Nyori. She knew they wouldn't let Lee-Tan do it. The Horse Band never really hurt their children. Still, she was glad when the old man spoke up.

"Me! I do it."

He turned down the offer of Torfinn's thick yew staff, taking instead a willow switch that was passed forward through the people. Carrying a firebrand in his other hand, he led Nyori and Anzeel away from the crowd, around a corner into a deep nook of the cave's great entrance chamber. There the people couldn't see them. Scratcher whipped them, the switch hissing in to loudly whap against Anzeel's leather trousers, then against Nyori's. The whipping hurt, yes, it did hurt a little, Nyori decided, meanwhile loudly screaming.

"Ouch! Oh! Oh! Ouch! Don't! Please!" Her moans, and Anzeel's, doubled and redoubled in echoes.

Scratcher was a joke among children of the Horse Band. Maybe he was just too feeble to hit hard. When he finished the punishment, Nyori could hear the rest of the people laughing, talking among themselves with renewed good humor. As the old man started back around the corner toward the group, Nyori grabbed his leather tunic and dragged him to a stop.

"I saw your winter horse, Scratcher, the furry one. I saw your cave lion," she said. "I liked the lion's eyes—the way you put light in them. Please, please, teach me to scratch in Deep Earth!"

His claw-marked old mouth turned downward in a frown.

"Irta's womb is sacred to men."

"Scratcher, you're the one who said it was sacred. You! How do you know?"

"Everyone knows! It came from the gods."

Nyori still held a leather handful of Scratcher's tunic when Anzeel took hold of hers, jerking impatiently at the sleeve.

"He's teaching *me* to make pictures," Anzeel said. "*Me*."

"But I'm better," she answered. "already better than you. That's what you said."

He had also said she was better than Scratcher. That she would not repeat just now.

"You're a girl," Anzeel groaned. "It's my turn."

"We don't have to take turns. Scratcher can teach me too."

She looked at the faces in the winking, smoky light of the firebrand—one face muddy but still fresh and smooth with its softly hairy lip, the other scarred and old. She saw sympathy in the eyes yet the mouths were level lipped, set against her. She jerked free of Anzeel's hand and stepped back.

"I went through Deep Earth," she yelled, "clear through it all the way. I saw more than our men ever saw. I saw more than you ever saw, Scratcher, more than Anzeel, because he didn't even look. I scratched a picture of the little colt we killed. I did it all, and nothing bad happened."

As if taking a blow, Scratcher expelled his breath in a grunt: "Huuuuh!" He breathed again and wiped his brow. "Irta be merciful! A girl scratched!"

"I told you it was wrong, Nyori," Anzeel mourned. He snuffled and wiped away tears that had risen in his eyes.

"Not in the Womb Shrine!" Scratcher said, almost pleading with the boy. "Not in the Womb Shrine?"

"No," Anzeel sobbed, "but it was bad."

This time it was not sorrowful tears that flooded Nyori, this time it was tears of rage. She gathered herself and screamed at them.

"Nothing happened! Nothing bad happened!"

Scratcher's eyes warily roamed the rocky nook, as if the next thing seen would be the bear that tore his body, the bear that killed Nyori's mother. He lifted his palms and opened them helplessly.

"When will it happen? We don't know."

Now it was Nyori who felt helpless and beaten and trapped.

"Yes, something bad will happen!" she shouted. "It always does. And when it happens next time, everyone will blame me."

6

Try Something Else

That year the warm wind had come early to the Land, breathing a mist of green through the trees, bringing blossoms out on crab apple and hawthorn. The Horse Band had come with it, eager for the hunt that would start as the big herds of horse and bison grazed up into the Blue Mountains under the Warm Sky sun. Now, to everyone's surprise, the Cold Sky turned gray and snow began falling.

For two days it blew fiercely across the Land. It built drifts in the ravines, drifts behind tree trunks, behind every boulder on the hillside below the cave, wind-carved into blue-white curves and domes and arches of ice. The people would stand shivering at the cave entrance to watch it, then move inside to warm themselves at the only fire the band kept burning. Already the fuel, firewood and reindeer bone, was in short supply. Already they had eaten the dried meat they carried from their last camp. With wintry light washing in from the cave mouth across his face, Torfinn waved out toward the falling snow.

"A girl in Deep Earth!" he snorted. "She brought this."

When snow stopped falling, the men loosened their sandal thongs, added a leather top, then took soft grasses from the beds they slept on and packed it around their feet for warmth. Over their heads they pulled sewn garments of hide with fur turned inward. As dawn brightened the cave mouth next morning, Scratcher led the winter-ready hunters out.

With the ground now frozen, the women could not dig for arrowhead and cattail tubers that grew along the river, nor for wild onions in nearby oak groves. They couldn't find acorns under the snow, nor thresh grasses or dried poppy heads or lentils for seed. Instead, they busied themselves patching clothing, splitting sinew to make sewing thread. They busied, busied themselves because they did not want to think that in truth they were only waiting. The sun was gone when the men came back exhausted, leather game bags hanging flat against their sides. For a long while, no one dared speak of the hunt. With empty bellies, the women huddled around the slow-burning fire. Weariest of all was Scratcher, who sat near the warmth rubbing his swollen knee joints. At last, eyes murky with shadows, he said:

"Bison didn't come. Nor reindeer."

Two days passed before they tried again. This time Anzeel's mother, Kansi, took up a lance and joined the hunt, walking beside her man, Drogben, and Anzeel, her son. He was truly her son but not Drogben's. Drogben's first woman had died while struggling to bear a child. Kansi's first man was killed when he darted under a mammoth and thrust a killing spear upward into the gut. The beast knelt on his chest. So Kansi and Drogben were together now, true mother and foster-father to Anzeel.

Nyori had prepared herself by fixing her own sandals with bedgrass for walking in the snow. She followed the hunters awhile at a distance, then ran to catch up. Torfinn raised his fist against her.

"Bad luck!" he growled. "She must go back."

"Leave her be!" Kansi yelled.

Nyori felt a rush of gratitude. So kind had Kansi been to Nyori that she called her foster-mother. Now she strode joyfully beside the woman. But when Anzeel reached out a hand to help her through a drift, she shook it off, feeling snow sift in among the grasses in her sandals.

"You're still mad at me, Nyori. Why are you mad?"

She just looked steadily back into his eyes, feeling as blank as the land around her. You're a girl, he'd said. Only a girl—never to be a

35

scratcher. Now she looked back at him but didn't answer.

Half blinded by the brilliance of sun on snow, they struggled all day through drifts and found almost nothing. Wanchuck caught a marmot far from its hole, ran it down and clubbed it—enough meat to feed four people. They found a patch of hazel shrubs hung with brown balls like dried flower petals. Inside the petal balls were hard shells and, within those, little nuts. They picked and cracked shells with their teeth, then crunched the nuts, rich with an oily sweetness.

"Eat one, save one," Scratcher reminded them.

It was an old rule. Those who had stayed behind in the cave must have a share. When the hazel nuts had all been picked, they staggered on through the snow, hungrier than ever for having eaten those few half-bites. They saw nothing big enough to feed the people—no horse, no bison, not even a deer or boar. With light going down the Sunset Sky, Anzeel suddenly threw his arm up, pointing at the cliff face ahead.

"Ibex!"

The goat looked like brown rock of the cliff, but its lean body and rainbow-curved horns stood out against one patch of snow. Anzeel and Drogben ran to the base of the cliff, spacing themselves wide apart one on either side of the goat. They climbed, clinging at cracks and knobs, catching at scrawny shrubs that grew out of the face. The women ran to stand close below them, anxious but silent.

Nyori watched Anzeel, sometimes moving her own hands and feet as he moved his on the crumbling face of the cliff. The ibex scampered lightly back and forth across the rock. He made Anzeel's and Drogben's slow crawling seem laughable. Yet when they came level with him, the animal finally realized he must escape past one of them.

Tiny hooves clattering on the rock, the ibex ran toward Anzeel, then stopped. He had caught the boy's scent. He turned to run across and steeply up the cliff face. This made a long throw for Drogben, who hung with one foot on a ledge, left arm crooked around a tree branch to steady himself. Nyori saw his right arm go back, the spear thrower level in his hand with its hook seated in the butt of the lance. Her eyes sucked at this sight, she wanted so badly to learn the powerful throw.

Drogben thrust up and violently forward, the thrower

lengthening his arm so the lance leaped out, flew like a hawk, its shadow racing over rock and snow. It pierced the running goat, struck through the chest, flint point jutting on the other side. Head craned back, Nyori saw the goat slump sideways, bounce down the rock and fall cleanly through the air, suddenly growing enormous in her sight. Kansi's arm jerked her backward.

WHAP!

The body struck the ground at Nyori's feet. The wooden shaft of the lance had snapped. Nyori grabbed the remaining butt, yanked it out and held it high, blood jetting hot from the wound to make a steamy porridge of the snow. The goat's amazed eye stared up at her, its legs jerking as if it still were dashing across the rock above. The tongue lolled bloody on the ice as the animal breathed its last.

"Yi-yeeeeeeeeee!" Nyori shrilled. "Drogben did it!" Nyori knew it was also Anzeel's victory, that they would have nothing except for Anzeel's skill in blocking the animal's escape. Still, she did not praise Anzeel.

Carried back to Owl Cave, the rank flesh of the male Ibex was roasted over a fire and divided, best cuts going to the smallest children and the two hunters who had taken it. Anzeel tried to share his extra portion with Nyori. She took some of that for Otti but refused the rest. Her own piece tasted smoky but delicious.

The whole thing made only one good meal for the Horse Band, and hunting continued bad.   Since the Mysteries had brought the children back, Scratcher invoked them again to bring bison and reindeer and red deer back to the Blue Mountains. For two days he stood with upraised arms at dawn and dusk, wiggling fingers to suck in spirits. No matter that the fingers flailed like bird wings, it didn't work. He said they would have to try something else.

7

How do you *do* this?

Something else? If making pictures helped hunters succeed, Nyori thought, why not a picture of the Ibex? That night, secretly, she carried an oil lamp into a dark recess of the cave's first chamber. Studying a bare wall patch, she recalled how the fallen ibex lay in the snow, its legs jerking in spasms as if still fleeing hunters. That's what she scratched, the dying animal with the butt of the lance still imbedded.

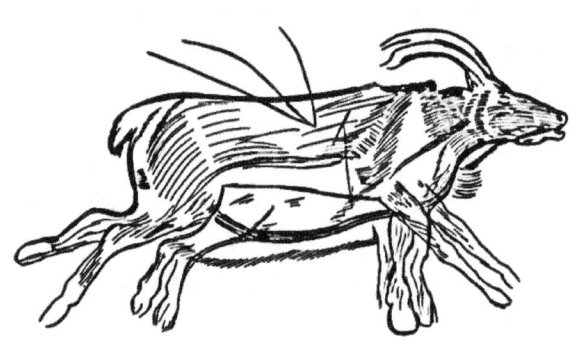

Her picture didn't change their luck. A few days after she scratched it, the men prepared to make hunting magic. In the entrance chamber near the Deep Earth Arch, Scratcher and Anzeel painted each other's faces with orange ocher. The red deer hide of Anzeel's new tunic had been tanned and chewed to wonderful softness by his mother, Kansi, but Nyori had sewn on the decoration of shells. Wearing it, he seemed to her more beautiful.

Usually the men enjoyed these ceremonies, waiting with

anticipation, socking each other, pushing and laughing and playing. Not this day. This day they only massaged their bellies hungrily, listening to the fretting of two babies. With nothing to eat themselves, the mothers were losing their milk. The babies pushed tiny hands at their mother's chests and wailed. Torfinn, darkly furious, stalked about the cave. He tossed his head scornfully.

"No magic when the cave is defiled. A girl saw Deep Earth! Women with their blood!"

Lee-Tan lay a hand on the cheek she herself had striped with scars.

"My son is right! Women's blood! Nyori made Irta angry by defiling Deep Earth. Now she defeats our hunting. Praise Irta! May Irta forgive us!" Nyori stared back at them with defiant eyes, frightened by their words but strangely thrilled. What if they knew she had scratched pictures in Deep Earth?

"She makes no blood," Drogben said. "She's too young , not a woman yet."

Kansi socked him on the shoulder—socked him hard.

"What's wrong with blood?" she wanted to know. "You've shed enough of it!"

Drogben had tried to say the right thing, tried to help Nyori. He shrugged and threw his hands out, baffled.

Kansi sat in the dust working flint. She had heated a head-sized chunk in the fire and quickly buried it, allowing the stone to cool slowly. That made the flint feel almost greasy to the touch and, more important, would make it split evenly. She hammered out a rough gray piece like a short section of tree trunk. Now she set a bone punch at the edge and struck the other end with a hammerstone, moved the punch and struck again: Ping! Ping! Ping! Spiraling it inward as, one by one, long flint blades fell away, peeling the lump toward its central core.

Each rough blade could be finely flaked to make a lance point or knife, scraper or burin or awl. Handled this way, a lump of precious flint could make many tools. This peeling operation was Kansi's specialty, requiring good eyes and a delicate touch. Kansi had the best eyes of all. Ping! Ping! She kept steadily at it until, once more, Torfinn took up his lament.

"She saw Deep Earth! She ruined us!"

This time Drogben rose and took hold of the man's pointed long nose, jerking it gently as he murmured.

"Shut up. I said, SHUT!"

Instantly, Torfinn obeyed, and Kansi's smile shone like the dawning sun on Drogben. In the man's face Nyori saw a flash of understanding: *Ah, so that's what she wants!* Watching the hairy man puzzle it out, Nyori felt a smile grow on her own lips.

Soon Scratcher called the men, welcoming the Hoppers as well as the few Shufflers among them. He told them Irta loves all styles of dancing. They trooped together through the Deep Earth Arch, hoping they could end the bad luck, bring animals back to the Blue Mountains.

By the fire Nyori found a piece of reindeer antler barely large enough to make the hook for a spear thrower. She studied the pinkish surface. Reindeer it was, but she saw a bison within it. The flint point of her burin slashed deeply, outlining the hump, then the curve of lower back sloping down—one cut, two, three on that line. She scraped and scraped until the scratch was deep enough to break away the material outside the figure. At last she had the profile of the animal's back.

Oh no! She sighed explosively. Now there was no room left for the head. She had worked herself into a trap. She had not done what her mother and Scratcher had taught her: At the start, always try to see the end. Breath grated in her throat. She tried to calm herself, to think of a bison grazing calmly, drifting slowly up a tundra hill. Now and again he swings his head back to lick the fly-bites on his hide, lick and lick at fly-bites. That's it! That's how she began to scratch it, cutting in the bison's head as he reached back to lick his flank. Antler flakes showered over her hands as she cut and polished, worked and worried the piece.

Nyori heard the distant rhythmic pounding of the hunters' drum in Deep Earth and idly wondered about them. Shade by shade, night darkened the cave entrance. The one fire burned down to embers. Someone lighted the braided-grass wick of a sandstone lamp, its flame drinking grease from a chunk of goat tallow. The people could have eaten the tallow, except they needed light. It flickered now across the folds and drapes of the cave ceiling, shone on the little figure that was taking final shape under her fingers.

She cut the bison's teardrop eye, the nostrils, the near-side horn curving up over the animal's forehead. Where would the far-side horn fit? She cut that in just below the high line of the hump. Next came many sharp slashes for a beard and the bristling mane above the shoulders. Then her breath hissed out again.

"Ssssst!" It was a failure. She realized the bison's hind leg wouldn't be strong enough to serve as hook for the spear thrower. It was all a waste! Cheeks burning, she set it aside, tried to think nothing more of it. Otti had been playing quietly with other children in a far corner of the chamber. Now he came toward her, dragging his sandals in the dust.

"Hungry!"

"I know."

"When eat?"

"Soon, Otti. Lie down." She patted the coarse fur of the robe.

He did as she said and quickly fell asleep, breathing noisily through an open mouth.   Nyori had forgotten the hollow drumming from Deep Earth, so regular and monotonous, noticing again only when it stopped. The men began pouring out through the Arch. They chattered nervously among themselves, laughing, waving their lances as they danced about, smiling into each others' eyes.

"Shufflers!" old Scratcher yelled, and all except Torfinn laughed as Scratcher shuffled.

"Hoppers!" shouted Drogben, demonstrating that he was one.

Torfinn stood scowling at this blasphemy before the gods, while Anzeel laughed with the other men. Then he came swiftly across to throw himself down beside her on the bison robe. His throat and arms were sweaty, flushed with color. He panted from his exertions in Deep Earth. She turned her face away, trying to feel the same blankness she had felt on the snowy hunt.

"You still mad at me?" he asked.

Instead of answering, she asked her own question.

"What did you do in Deep Earth?"

He looked at the ground and smiled.

"I'm not supposed to tell."

"Kansi knows," Nyori said.

Reminded of his mother, he swung his eyes to Kansi, who was seated beside Drogben far away beside the fire. Already she had wetted

41

her man's cheeks with water and was shaving his whiskers with a finely-flaked blade. No one else sharpened blades as keenly as Kansi did. Among all the men, Drogben was most particular about how he looked. He was hairy everywhere else but didn't like a scraggly, messy beard. When the Kansi's eyes met Nyori's, she flashed a smile. Kansi liked to see these two young people together, and Nyori knew why.

The story of Shufflers and Hoppers was often told to show how beliefs could split one people into hateful factions. But Scratcher also told another story showing how two different peoples could become one. That story came to him from his mother. Many winters ago—even before Shufflers and Hoppers—the Horse Band formed when a family of blue eyes and a family of brown eyes joined.

The gods ordained that blue boys and girls could not be together, nor brown boys and girls. The gods wanted brown with blue and blue with brown. So the story had come down the generations. By now the brown family had blue members, and the same the other way. Brown and blue were all mixed up. But everyone knew brothers and sisters, even cousins, must not be together.

Nyori did not believe in the gods, but she understood this exchange of boys and girls between families did make for peace within bands. Peace, even, between horse folk and other bands of the Steppe People, because exchanges between bands were considered good—family ties giving people good reasons not to fight. She was pleased that her brown eyes and Anzeel's blue allowed his mother to smile approvingly when they were together, as now. Around them the cave filled with the sleepy murmur of the people. Though no one was listening, Anzeel lowered his voice.

"You already know about Deep Earth ceremonies. Why do I have to tell it?"

She looked full into his eyes. His cheeks reddened even more, she could see it in the lamplight. Was it him she liked, or the patterned shells she had sewn on the tunic across his chest? He sank down on one elbow, moving his face so close she could feel his breath as he spoke.

"All right. We just scratched new pictures of horse and bison. All the hunters went back to dance. Rothgar kept rhythm by pounding on a bison shoulder blade, and I played my flute. With the new picture and all the other pictures around, it was wonderful. We're making the animals come, we're *making* them." Under her steady, skeptical gaze, he blinked. "It does! It makes them come!" he said, and then sighed. "You don't believe. Why?"

"I believe what I see."

"You're not answering."

"Anzeel, you know why."

"About your mother dying? And Scratcher couldn't help her? My father was killed too, Nyori. That mammoth killed him, a mammoth like the one Irta rides. *I believe*."

Staring into his earnest face, his sweet face, her eyes seemed to burn in their sockets.

"Why? *Why* do you believe, if Irta controls everything and she let your father die?"

Anzeel lay his right hand on the breast of his tunic.

"Because I feel her. I feel Irta here."

"Well I don't!"

She felt suffocatingly warm inside herself, wanting either to be closer to him or farther away. His face was dirty. He was just a dirty-faced boy. She moved away on the fur. He slapped the hide with his open hand, making dust fly.

"I know why you're mad at me. You're jealous because I make pictures in Deep Earth."

She felt sullen, a lump of firestone weighting her belly.

"You get to hunt," she said.

"Well, most women can't hunt because they have babies. My mother hunts. You hunt."

"But the men teach you how to use the spear thrower. You do everything. You even try to boss me like all the men boss the women."

"I'll teach you the thrower, Nyori."

She turned her back on him.

"Leave me alone."

She could still feel him there, a slow-burning fire that warmed her back.

"You say men are bosses," he told her, "but we have to have *something* all our own. Women are powerful. We all come out of women's bellies, men and women and everybody, out between your legs. Men can't make babies. And I want you more than you want me, Nyori. You've got all the power over me. Look at me now, I'm over here begging. You never beg me."

Neither did most of the men beg their women for anything. Anzeel was one of the few. Nyori liked him for that, and did not like him for it.

"I begged you to let me learn pictures in Deep Earth."

"Nyori, I can't!".

"You could take my side."

She sat there feeling his presence behind her, hearing the silence of him. Then he said:

"What's this?"

She swung around. The useless spear thrower hook lay across his two hands. She didn't want to think about it—how she had weakened the leg, the vital hook of the thrower.

"Nothing," she sighed. "It's no good, hook's not strong."

"You just scratched this," he said, "scratched it while we were in Deep Earth?"

"Yes. It's no good."

His eyes kept blinking shut and opening wide again. Misty eyed, he looked at the dry piece of antler as if it were a precious chunk of firestone, the tenderloin of boar, as if in it he could see Irta and the Mysteries and all the other gods. This caused Nyori to look again.

"It *is* good, Nyori. It's good! Who cares if the hook isn't strong? It can be the weight at the end of the thrower, to give it power."

His words cheered her, but Anzeel himself looked tragic stricken. He lay the piece on the hide between them.

With the palms of both hands, he pounded the sides of his head.

"How do you *do* this? How? Why can't *I* do it? Nyori, I'm never going to be a scratcher! Never!"

He jumped to his feet. Nyori sat there feeling the warmth die away as he fled swiftly across the chamber toward his mother and Drogben.

"Anzeel, if you like the bison, you can have it. Come back!"

He did not come back.

8

Run, Cave Brow, run!

A human figure slowly rose above the hill crest, first head and shoulders, then the squat body, laboring mightily as it floundered through snowdrifts. The man struggled to run, glancing back over his shoulder. With his short legs and swinging arms, he seemed ill suited for deep snow yet moved with amazing speed.

Nyori saw he was from the Cave Brows, people whose eyes nested deep under the ledge of their back-sloped foreheads like owl eyes staring from a cave. They were great mammoth hunters, powerful fighters at close quarters, but they used only clumsy spears. They had never learned the thrower. Scratcher told an old story that Cave Brows were the Ancients' ancestors, that Cave Brows had once been the only people of the Land. Now just a tiny band survived, hidden in one canyon of the Blue Mountains.

When the man fled down the hill toward her, Nyori slipped easily into the cover of a pine thicket. Cave Brows were mostly good people. Still, she had to be careful. She drew her fur top close, her moist breath riming its collar with frost.

She had awakened late that morning to find the Horse Band hunters already gone, Kansi with them. She grabbed up her own lance and tried to follow but lost them at a crossing of snow-tramped trails. Still she hadn't found them, and the sun was halfway down the Sunset Sky, casting black shadows in footprints that stretched behind the Cave Brow. Why was the man struggling so hard to run? She let her eyes follow his trail back to the hill crest. Her surprised breath shot out in steam.

Men moved there on the snow, a band of warriors. They had crossed the hillcrest and now loped down along the Cave Brow's track. Just from numbers alone, it had to be Wolf-Kills. No other band had so many warriors. She sank deeper into the thicket, parting branches with her hands to see out. Most of them wore simple hats of fur, but those in the lead wore headdresses of wolf skulls with upper jaws, the fangs projecting above their faces. They were lean men, looking hungrier than the Horse People, maybe because bison had not come to them either.

The swiftest gained steadily on the Cave Brow, who had veered downhill toward a cluster of high rocks projecting from the hillside. Yes, Nyori thought, he can hole up there, use angles of stone to protect himself from their long throws, making them come close to reach him. Close up, he would hold his own against any of them, maybe against all of them. She felt her cold hands clench eagerly. Run, Cave Brow, run!

Suddenly the lead Wolf-Kill stopped on the sun-dazzled snow, hauled back his arm with thrower poised and launched a lance. It arched upward, flew far, struck quivering into the snow ahead of the Cave Brow, who jerked it up as he ran—a second weapon for him to use. Then other Wolf-Kills began stopping to throw. Lances rained down behind the Cave Brow, beside him, ahead of him—more than he could pick up and carry, though he grabbed several more as he struggled forward. Nyori groaned. He would never reach the rocks. She saw him spin on his track and stop. Now, at least, he could dodge their lances. He raised his own heavy spear to threaten his pursuers. They fanned out in a half-circle and moved slowly inward.

She wanted to believe they would not do it. How could they? But of course they would. It was their belief. Even if the Horse Band's Irta did not exist, at least she was a god of goodness. The Wolf-Kill's Irta made them do terrible things. In following Irta they were fierce as wolves and so killed wolves to make their costumes. They killed each other in arguments over who loved Irta most, who had sacrificed most. They killed just to prove their love of the god. Real wolves seldom killed except to eat. Wolf-Kills did because their Irta wanted blood. All this the Cave Brow knew well enough. That's why he had fled before them.

"Irta, Irta, Irta," Nyori muttered, not believing yet unable to keep shut about her.

The Cave Brow's lone shadow stretched out far behind him on the snow, a wide array of shadows closing toward it. He held his own brute spear in his right hand but abruptly raised the left, brandishing the lances he had picked up. He would die now, he knew that, yet his voice floated faintly up across the snow to Nyori.

"Ha! Haaah!" Laughing gruffly that they had so uselessly thrown away their weapons.

He had their lances but no thrower that would let him reach them. The enemies arrayed around him methodically fitted their own throwers into the sockets of yet more lances. Nyori let supple needles of the pine branches close before her eyes, then fell face down in the snow. It melted against her eyelids. She breathed warmly into it and licked moisture with her tongue.

If I were brave, if I were like Drogben, she thought, I would leap up now and burst out of this thicket. I would shout, "Stop! Stop, you Wolf-Kills." I have a lance. I could stop them. "Stop you Wolf-Kills." These last words she actually whispered into the snow against her face.

A sudden clamor of voices rose to her from the hillside below, like snow geese clanging across the winter sky—such an innocent sound. She didn't want to hear it. She pushed her face deeper into snow, biting great mouthfuls to stop herself from crying out, swallowing snow water as it gathered around her tongue.

Nyori had seen Cave Brows at gatherings on the plain, where they traded raw mammoth ivory for fancy creations of the Horse Band women—beaded garments, cordage and rope and little animals made from the very ivory the Cave Brows themselves had traded away the year before. She thought Cave Brow children were the prettiest of all children. Their eyes were warm with light, eyes like Anzeel's blue ones, set deep amid the delicate bones of their faces. Nyori had made eyes at their child eyes as they hid behind their mothers. She won their trust and was privileged to toss them giggling into the air, tossing and catching and tossing until they and she could no longer endure the delight.

With her face buried in wet coldness, Nyori waited so long she thought it must be over. Surely by now it would over and the Wolf-Kills gone. But when she looked out through the branches again, blood splashed the snow where the Cave Brow had made his stand. The Wolf-Kills were just moving away, back up the hill from which they came.

Four of them dragged the Cave Brow, two on each leg, hauling him feet first through the snow, the trail behind him blood spattered. Four others dragged a bison hide on which a second man lay. Blood came from him, too, a thin red line against the white. All the Wolf-Kills together had slaughtered the Cave Brow. Somehow, by himself, he had killed one of them.

Nyori stood up and pushed her way through pine branches, pushed into the open, standing boldly there with sun warm on her face. She wanted them to see her. She wanted to yell at them, yell defiance, "Ha! Haaaaah!" as the Cave Brow had yelled. She bit the web of flesh between her thumb and forefinger to stifle the cry. The Wolf-Kills never looked back as they marched up the hill.

Nyori turned away, pushed through the pine thicket to the far side and hurried toward Owl Cave, walking and running, sometimes falling full length in the snow, only to rise up and stagger on, now screaming again and again what she should have screamed aloud at the murderers.

"Stop, you Wolf-Kills! Stop!"

The sun was well down when she saw the cave mouth ahead of her. It was only then that the meaning of it came to her. For five summers the Wolf-Kills had been gone from the Blue Mountains. Now they were back. So a new bad thing had happened for the Horse Band, the second bad thing since she scratched her first big picture in Deep Earth.

Panting from her run, Nyori ran into the cave and told the Band what had happened. The people set up a shout. Rothgar ran for his lance and battle axe, as if the killers at that moment might charge in through the cave mouth. This set off the other men, who also armed themselves and milled about the cave. Women wailed, frightening their own children into wild screaming.

At first Lee-Tan and Torfinn stood shivering and pale near the entrance, their faces showing strange half-smiles. Nyori saw they were glad, *glad*, the Wolf Kills had returned. Lee-Tan spoke to her son. When he grabbed up his oaken staff, it was not to protect them all from Wolf-Kills.

Nyori felt herself seized by the wrist, heard the hiss of the staff, pain flaming in her legs as heavy oak whacked flesh. She flinched and danced away, screaming. Amid all the other yelling, no one heard her cries—no one except Otti, whose face twisted up in terror as he saw his sister beaten. She tried to fight away from Torfinn but was paralyzed by his grip, which almost broke her wrist.

"Evil!" he screamed. "You Evil! You always brought bad luck."

She tried to shield her body with one hand, the staff popping loudly, bloodying her knuckles, burning her palm when she tried to catch it. The oak lashed her legs, slashed her body, beating and beating her flesh. She saw faces of the people turning toward them, beginning to notice. Desperately Nyori searched the crowd for Anzeel and Drogben, despairing when she remembered they had gone hunting together. What she did see was Scratcher's scarred face coming around, the mouth dropping open as he reacted.

"What? What? You beat our children!"

"Keep back, Evil!" Torfinn shouted.

"Irta-betrayer!" Lee-Tan screamed at him. She began to shuffle, turning in a little circle, raising her hands to the rock above. "Praise Irta, punish the Evil!"

Scratcher raised hands before him and walked straight toward Torfinn, as if to pacify him. The butt of the staff struck out, knocked Scratcher onto his back. He lay there writhing. Before Torfinn could raise the staff again, Kansi rushed him, bounced back from his chest, then stood screaming at him.

"You're crazy! You're crazy, beating little girls!"

Torfinn knocked her down, stepped boldly forward and stood over her, panting. He closed his fist around Nyori's hair, dragged her across Kansi's prostrate figure and displayed her to the crowd, violently shaking her head.

"She angered Irta! Went through Deep Earth! She is the Evil. Scratcher is the Evil. That's why he lies for her."

"We let the Hopper lead us!" Lee-Tan yelled, still shuffling in her circle. "He sends a girl to Irta's womb! That's why we're starving!"

With her head twisted aside by his grip on her hair, Nyori glanced up to see Anzeel appear suddenly against the flare of light from the cave mouth. Drogben marched in behind him, bent over from the weight of the red deer he carried across his shoulders. Blood from the animal's opened body had splashed his garment. With a mighty grunt, Drogben shrugged the load up over his head and let it fall.

"This time Anzeel killed it!" Drogben announced, laying his arm around the boy's shoulders. "Short throw, but the deer was running full out. He has a good arm."

They were grinning, both of them. Having stepped from the white blaze of snow outside, they blinked in the dimness, blinder than Scratcher, bewildered as they began to make out faces not joyous at the promise of fresh meat but, instead, more nearly tragic. Torfinn dragged Nyori three steps forward so he could stand over the deer carcass, as he had stood over Kansi.

"See! See!" He swept his free arm wide in a possessive gesture above the deer, as if he himself had brought it home. "We whip the Hopper Evil, and Irta gives meat!"

He let go of her hair, moving with slow dignity back toward his place in the cave, a well-planned move on his part, Nyori decided. By the time Drogben and Anzeel found out what had happened, they didn't know what to do, and so did nothing. The Horse Band didn't beat their children. But because hunting was bad, because the Wolf-Kills had returned to the Blue Mountains, they had let Torfinn blame Nyori and beat her. He beat Nyori, he struck down Scratcher and Kansi, and no one did anything. He was powerful, suddenly more powerful than Drogben, more powerful than Scratcher. Nyori marveled that the man who loved Wolf-Kills, who followed their god, now could use fear of them to dominate her people.

Grinning crazily, Otti straddled Anzeel's chest, reaching down to slap the older boy's face, or seem to slap him, for the gesture was more like a caress.

"I slap, I slap you!" the little boy giggled.

"I slap you back!" growled Anzeel, reaching up as if to do it but only rocking the child's head back and forth, cradling the little dome of skull between his hands.

Bluish light from the cave mouth paled Anzeel's eyes yet somehow deepened them. Nyori glanced quickly away from him, turning to look out. The snowstorms had stopped, but the ground still lay deeply covered. The hunters had given up for this day. With little to eat, everyone tired easily, everyone except Anzeel.

"Wu-ho!" he said. "Ride the reindeer! Wu-ho!"

Yet again he bucked the child on his belly. Anzeel was good with her Otti, who was upset by what had happened to his sister. Anzeel was trying to comfort him by playing hitting games that didn't hurt. Now the distraction failed, Otti's grin vanished and once more the little face twisted into a worried mask.

"He hit sister," Otti whined. "Hurt Nyori. Torfinn did."

"I know, Otti," Anzeel said.

"Torfinn hits."

"I know. But she's better now."

It was everybody's bison robe, everybody's robe to sit on at the cave mouth, and it was nobody's robe, so nobody ever shook it out. Dust puffed up as Anzeel set Otti off and slid closer to Nyori. He lay his hand on the calf of her leg, a cold hand but pleasant, two fingers resting lightly over the scabby red welt just above her ankle. The back of her body was thick with welts like that. For two days afterward, they had hurt so fiercely she couldn't sleep. Now they smarted only when she stretched the skin by moving suddenly.

"Sorry I wasn't here," Anzeel said. He'd said this several times before.

"You couldn't stop it. Kansi couldn't. Even Scratcher couldn't stop it."

Outside the sky was clearing, a raven flapping lazily across, aimlessly rising and falling as it flew toward distant woods. Nyori looked down and tried to focus on the picture she was scratching, a red deer doe on a red deer shoulder blade. This was fresh bone, soft and easy to scratch, yet she could not concentrate. She couldn't get her mind off what had happened.

Exhausted from his fretting, Otti by now had fallen asleep on the dusty bison robe. Now Anzeel moved closer to Nyori, put his hands out and let them rest on her waist. Feeling the pull of him, she laid hands lightly on his chest—not to hold Anzeel away, more to hold herself back.

"I don't believe in Irta," she said.

"Shhhhhh. Don't let them hear." His glance flew around the cave. Torfinn and Lee-Tan sat beside a guttering oil lamp near the far wall, heads together and talking. They had not heard Nyori's remark, but she lowered her voice anyway.

"When Scratcher talks about her, Irta is good. When Torfinn does, she's evil. It's all in who's talking."

So urgent was he to convince her that his hands tightened on her waist, giving her pain that was almost pleasure.

"*I* believe," he said. "It's right to believe in Irta, it's right when Irta's good."

They would never agree—never, never. Just because of it, they caught themselves smiling broadly into each other's eyes. She hugged him fiercely to her and instantly pushed him away. Then Nyori's mouth corners dragged downward in a frown. She looked back into Anzeel's eyes and saw his grin also had died. Like her, he couldn't get his mind off Torfinn's attack

"What are we going to do?" he asked her.

She grabbed up the red deer shoulder bone on which she'd been scratching. Violently, she hurled it at the cave wall, where it chipped rock before glancing into dirt.

"I don't know," she told him. "I don't know what *we're* going to do."

9

Scratcher Woman

That night she prepared a fresh wick of bedgrass for an oil lamp, then lay down beside Otti in her cave nook as if to sleep. They lay together, listening to sleepy murmurs of the people, to their coughing, to long sighs as they settled down. Without even looking, she sensed where Anzeel lay far away near his mother and Drogben. For a long time now she had been able to feel his presence even at a distance. She pushed her lips close against her brother's ear.

"Otti, after you go to sleep, I will leave for awhile. If you wake, don't yell for me."

"I go? Go with?"

"No."

"I want *go-o-o*, sis, please please."

Her breath hissed out in a sigh of surrender. Since the Wolf-Kills had returned, the Horse Band had begun posting a guard. Tonight it was Rothgar. Nyori waited till he stepped outside. One fire smoldered dimly, one lamp flickered, but the chamber was thick with shadow. By then she had to shake Otti awake. She took his hand and pulled him up.

"Go Deep Earth?" he whispered.

He was dumb, but in his way he was smarter than anyone else Nyori knew. She tugged him slowly across the chamber, paused for a moment before the Deep Earth Arch, taking a long breath as if she were again about to swim the river that came out of the hill. Heart pounding, pulling Otti along, she ducked through.

"Can't see-eee."

"Shhhhhhh."

They felt their way forward taking breaths of earthy air, scraping knees on gravel even through their leather trousers, until Nyori could no longer see the faintest light from behind. She drew out the bedgrass wick and, with flint and firestone, struck sparks to light it. From a tallow lump, fire melted grease, which soaked into the wick and burned with a smoky flame. Holding Otti's sticky hand with one of her own, carrying the sandstone lamp in the other, she moved ahead.

Soon the animals began to appear, living intensely here on the walls—boar pig and reindeer, everywhere bison and horses, the best-loved animals of the Horse Band. They turned to the right and threaded through a down-sloping, wet-clay passage, angling their bodies to avoid a dripping ledge. The passage opened into a dry chamber both wide and high, where rock hung above in jagged points, sharp-edged folds.

Here it was, the Womb Shrine, where animals were thickest, animal atop animal in spiderwebs of scratching. Here stood Nyori in Irta's womb, but it was not the gods she felt around her. She felt instead the Scratchers, felt their human presence here as she often felt Anzeel's. Him she could feel over distance; these people she felt through ages of time, not as men or women but as Scratchers, the mothers and fathers of her people. Felt them as a warmth inside herself. Here in the Womb Shrine, sacred of sacred, she would scratch—but not *over* their pictures. That she could not endure. Nyori searched the chamber and found an empty patch high up like a bit of wall hanging from the ceiling.

"Me with lamp, Nyori. Lemme, lem-meeee."

That he wanted to help pleased her. Adding another lump of fat, she placed the lamp in his hands. She climbed a sloping ledge to reach the bare patch. Here the rock was surface cracked but firm beneath, just right for her first big bison. She thought about Scratcher's powerful winter stallion on the cave wall. She thought also of the little bison she'd shaped from reindeer antler, reaching back to lick its flank.

This would be different from either, a huge bull bison she had seen the summer before grazing down a hill of sweetgrass. The bison's head jerks up as he hears another animal bawling. What other animal? The bison wonders.

She lay her flint burin on the stone and drew it smoothly to the right, black flecks falling from the point. She stood well back with arm extended so the line would flow, rising where the bull neck thickened. Her bison raised its nose high, light shining from the dark center of the eye, its head shaded to show delicate bones of the muzzle, stiff hairs curving forward under the line of its jaw. She scratched his head turned a little so both twice-curved horns would show, indicating not the flatness of rock but endless depths of the world above. He stood with his tongue thrust out, bawling back at that other animal.

But *what* other animal? Nyori wasn't yet sure. She decided for this picture it was fall and rutting season for all the hoofed creatures. Nyori knew bison, how they tossed their tree-stump heads when stinging flies bothered them, throwing strings of drool across their shedding backs. She loved bison, their force, the gamy smell of them as the herd rumbled past. So far she'd finished only head and neck and shoulders.

But by now her bison had guessed—so Nyori decided—that the other animal was a red deer stag. So, starting just at the base of her bison's neck she scratched the stag, also bawling with tongue out, as if he were only the bison's thought, a huge thought, like a red deer the bison had seen long ago and now called up in his mind, the stag bawling as the bison bawled in imitation.

The Ancients never showed grass or ground beneath their animals. In this she followed their lead, she honored the Ancients. Then Nyori crawled down from her perch and stood back to see. Otti stood with her, wide eyes gleaming, biting the pink tip of his tongue between white teeth.

"Hold the lamp higher," she told him.

The bison's head showed only faintly against the stone, so thin were the lines that surrounded it. She crawled up again to scratch in the animal's shaggy coat, the upstanding stiff mane on the neck and hump. But already she was beginning to despair—just as she'd despaired in carving her little reindeer antler bison. She'd made another awful mistake—scratched the bison so big she had no room to sketch in his body. And she'd made the stag's front hooves big and clumsy. Still, she worked on till her hand ached from gripping the jagged flint, till her ears wearied of scritch-scritch-scritch—the same sound Scratcher made when thoughtfully stroking his bristly chin. For some reason, everything around her seemed clearer and brighter now. Then Otti's voice drifted up from below.

"Anzeel," he grumbled, "I sleepy. You hold mine?"

Nyori spun around on the ledge, nearly falling off. Anzeel stood below, staring up at her picture with his mouth open. If a bug came past, it could fly right in. He held his own lamp high, Otti tugging at his hand.

"*An-zeel*, hold mine!"

He took Otti's lamp without looking down. He kept staring at her picture with his stupid open mouth. Nyori threw her burin not quite at him. He flinched as it struck the floor beyond his feet and skittered to the wall.

"Why did you have to follow me!" she yelled. Anzeel's mouth snapped shut. He set Otti's lamp on the floor, turned and strode back through the cave, lifting a hand to shield his head where the dripping ledge forced him to lean. "Why do you follow me?" she yelled again. "Why?" yelling pointlessly, because in another moment even the glow of Anzeel's lamp dimmed and then vanished in the blackness of the passage. She crawled down to get the burin, relieved to find it wasn't broken. Agitated, she stared into the darkness of the passage, trying to see what might be coming.

"He won't tell on me," she muttered. "He won't tell. I know he won't." She looked at Otti as if expecting him to answer. He blinked sleepily. The only sound was a sharp drip-drip-drip from the ledge. "I have to finish," she told herself.

She worked a long time cutting in the bison's round eye, the details of the muzzle, finely shaping the twin lines of the bison's horns and its left ear. She scratched in the coarse hair on the animal's shoulder. All her life she'd watched as bisons were butchered and so knew not just outer skin but layer on layer underneath of muscle and bone and shining gut. She bent the hair to show the curve of flesh as flesh was shaped by underlying bone.

She still felt sad that she couldn't finish her bison. She hadn't left space for it! But now, at least, she liked the scritch-scritching of her flint, liked the noise because she wanted to hear nothing else. But at last she admitted to herself she did hear other sounds: the scraping of many feet against the floor of the passage, throat coughs and grunting. Then came flickers of light, gleaming and dimming in the passage, the light of many lamps.

Nyori sat down on the ledge so she wouldn't fall. Air rasping in her throat, she lay one hand on the leather tunic above her heart, trying to contain its wild beating. Seeing his sister's fright, Otti crouched in a corner and started crying. Lamp in hand, Anzeel came out first and moved to stand below her and beside Otti. Behind him came Torfinn, carrying a mammoth-hide shield and lance. Torfinn!

"Aaaaaah!" he wailed. "The Evil! Woman in Womb Shrine! Evil scratching!" With one arm holding his lance at mid shaft, he raised it high to shake at Nyori.

Others filed in to gather below her, Rothgar and Wanchuck and Sudrog. One figure wore a reindeer costume, black horns towering above his head, with only the stringy old human neck to reveal it as Scratcher. Drogben wore his horse disguise. Dressed for ceremony, for battle or for killing—Nyori didn't know which—they all carried weapons as they crowded into a chamber ablaze with lamps. Anzeel stared up with a frown on his face, the face Nyori so many times had touched. She screamed at him.

"You told on me! You had to be so jealous of my scratching! Oh, Anzeel, you told on me! You told, you told!"

In flickering lamplight Torfinn turned to face the men, shuffling feet in the dust and raising shield in one hand, lance in the other.

"Hopper Evil dirtied Irta's womb. The god is angry!"

"No!" Scratcher shouted, his voice hollow inside the mask. "Irta is grateful tonight for what the child has done."

"He lies!" Torfinn said, shuffling, shuffling in his stupid circle. "Her womb is violated, but Irta forgives when we kill the Evil. Praise Irta!"

Nyori saw that Drogben, powerful Drogben, stood far back in the crowd—too distant to stop it even if he wanted to. They let Torfinn beat me with his staff, she thought. Will they also let him kill me?

"No!" Scratcher shouted. "Irta is glad because today she gave birth. Our Nyori is born, born again as Irta's child, beloved child of earth."

He began hopping, bouncing up and down as if to counter Torfinn's shuffling. He's crazy, Nyori thought, they're *all* crazy. Torfinn jerked to a stop, planting his feet. She saw the lance slide forward through his fist as he felt for the right grip, saw his arm cock itself for the throw. This close, there was no need for the spear-thrower. She flinched back against the stone, against her Bawling Bison, raising hands to shield her face.

He wouldn't need to kill her, she would die from the pounding of her heart, just from hearing Otti's frightened shrieks. Panting wildly, she waited for the flint's vicious bite and, when death did not come, jerked hands apart to see a slight figure—Anzeel!—hanging from Torfinn's cocked right arm, wrestling with it. The horned reindeer swept behind the two, frail arms snaking out from the furry robe to choke in on Torfinn's neck.

Three figures swayed together there, the furious dance of their feet stirring a lamplit cloud of dust. They swayed and then collapsed to the floor. Drogben did not help the old man and the boy, nobody helped them. But with Anzeel and Scratcher on top, Torfinn struggled, then sagged and raised one hand up into the dust cloud.

"Irta...Irta..." he moaned.

Anzeel bounced on his chest. Torfinn coughed and shut up. Scratcher yanked the man's lance away and stood up disgustedly, as if stepping away from a rotting carcass, an animal long dead on the ground.

"Irta is angry!" Torfinn moaned.

"Yes!" Scratcher said. "At you. That's why she stopped you from killing Nyori. So brave a fighter against women." He turned to the men. "This is a sign. Believe!"

He grabbed Torfinn's arm and dragged the man to his feet, pushing him back toward the passage leading to the cave mouth.

"Evil!" Torfinn shrieked.

He kept yelling it as he grabbed up a lamp and shuffled away down the passage, his voice fading with every turn. Despite the noise, Otti had stopped crying, somehow sensing the change. Scratcher turned his eyes on the men but threw his arm up toward Nyori.

"Look!" he shouted, his voice hollow within the mask.

The others stared at her—no, not at *her*. Lifting their lamps high, they stared at the bison and the stag behind her on the wall. She was too close herself to get a good look at the scratching. She jumped down from the ledge and turned to see. Scratcher now raised both arms.

"Look!" he said again, as if they were not already looking. "As the boy told us, her creatures live! Her stag calls, and the bison answers. They live on the wall! This is better than my father's scratching, better than mine." The old man's eyes squinted so furiously through the murky light that Nyori wondered whether he could even see the bison. But he shouted:

"This, *this* is praise to Irta! Nyori honors Irta, her Mother-God!"

I don't, she thought, I don't either! But was her picture really good? She stood among them and turned her own eyes up to see.

It wasn't finished, but...maybe it wasn't so bad.

On her bare shoulders she felt the prickly hairs of Scratcher's reindeer robe as he moved behind her. His hands came down cold on her shoulders, squaring them back, turning her to face the hunters. Their eyes glanced downward from the picture to her face, up from her face to the picture, down to her face again. Surprise shone in all those eyes. Scratcher's bony hands squeezed her shoulders as he presented her before them. picture, down to her face again. Surprise shone in all those eyes. Scratcher's bony hands squeezed her shoulders as he presented her before them.

"I am Scratcher man," he said. "Old, nearly blind, I die soon. Then Nyori will be Horse Band Scratcher. Scratcher Woman."

His hands propelled her forward into the midst of them, the men falling back, smiling shyly, looking at the ground. They didn't know what was expected of them.

"Give her welcome!" Scratcher boomed.

As a flush of embarrassment heated her face, Nyori wished they would do *something*. At last Drogben said, "Ha!" and stepped close. She thought he would grab her as before, grab her and lift and shake her like red meat salmon. No. With an open hand rough as treebark, he boxed her lightly on the cheek, then made a fist and clunked the top of her head. "Ha!" he barked. Other hands came out to sock her shoulder, slap her back, tickle her ribs, pull her nose, wag one ear back and forth. "Ho!" Wanchuck grunted. "Ha!" With calloused thumb and forefinger, Rothgar sampled the smoothness of her chin.

"Whiskers? If she be Scratcher, she needs whiskers."

They all laughed. Though it didn't seem funny, she laughed too. They slapped her and poked her, shoulder bumped and butt bumped her. With their deep belief in Irta, they had stood by moments before while Torfinn prepared to kill her. They might themselves have killed her.

Now strange feelings grew like tree roots between her and every one of them. She had long been a darling of the Horse Band, as all children were. She had been the darling of Anzeel, the darling of his desire, he wanting her more than she wanted him. But this with the men of the band, this was different, a fellow feeling, Nyori becoming one with them—though still a girl, or perhaps woman.

Anzeel—where, she wondered, was Anzeel? He was standing outside all this, back near the entrance passage, a slim figure leaning on his lance shaft. She had won out over Anzeel. She, Nyori, would be

Scratcher—not he. She tried to fight back the sense of triumph that dizzied her, surging up with the blood pounding through her brain.

The men around her were socking each other, laughing and patting and pushing each other. Nyori slipped through them and moved close to Anzeel, tried to stand where his eyes were looking. He looked away. Struggling to control the jubilant blood that clouded her vision, she said:

"Anzeel, I was afraid you would tell on me."

"That's what I did," he said. "I told." If a dead man could talk, he would speak in such a voice.

"You told them my bison was good," Nyori said. "You saved me from Torfinn."

Dead his voice might be, but she saw how his heart beat strongly under the tunic, torn at the neck, dust smeared from the fight. The knuckles of his hand dripped blood. She reached out to touch that wrist. Anzeel jerked his hand away and stepped back from her.

"Scratcher wants you," he said. "He wants you to make hunting magic."

She covered her mouth with one hand, hissing words through the fingers.

"Anzeel, I *can't* My magic won't work! What will they do to me when it doesn't work?"

He only nodded toward the group behind her.

"Scratcher wants you."

10

Her Magic!

It was midday, but there was no sun—not even the slightest special brightness anywhere above. Dirty snow rolled away into far distance, where a gray horizon melted upward into gray sky. They tramped through it, Nyori carrying a lance and a thrower she didn't know how to use. She and Scratcher marched on the left of the hunters' line. All day they had paced the hunt together.

"What happens if we don't see bison?" she asked him.

"We will. You made powerful magic in Deep Earth."

"If we don't, what happens to *me?*"

One of his hands cupped the back of her head while the other gently closed her mouth, his bloodshot eyes looking into hers.

"Stop talk. I lived long as Scratcher. It didn't always work for me."

He said nothing more, just turned his eyes to the front and picked his way between clumps of hazel bush, no nuts hanging on the bare branches of this patch. Of course, Scratcher couldn't know what the hunters would do if her magic failed. Believing in Irta, believing in all the gods, they might do anything.

A long hill rose before them, rose gradually into a faraway sky. The slope was thick with grass and shrubs. Just ahead, a line of trees followed a creek valley that angled across it. As they climbed, the hunters had spread themselves in a half-moon curve across the hillside, sagging backward in the middle. Drogben and Anzeel ranged far out on the right keeping watch, since the Wolf-Kill camp lay in that direction. If the advancing line flushed horse or bison, the animals would be forced to escape around the horns of the half-moon. But the people were weak from hunger, light headed and slow moving. Nyori's own belly felt hollow with hunger. How could they overtake fast-running animals?

She hoped they would at least see a herd before nightfall. It had seemed silly to her, yesterday's Deep Earth ceremony, hunters dancing wildly around figures she had shaped on the cave floor. This had happened just after Torfinn's defeat. Because the men liked its meat best of all, they wanted her to make a another bison. When she protested she'd just made one on the wall, they laughed. The old man smiled as if pleased that, though a good Scratcher, she yet had much to learn.

"Works only if we dance while you make it," he told her.

"All right," she sighed, but this time she wanted something different. She led them deeper into the cave, far into a darkness that livened with the flare and dip of lamplight, then died to darkness and silence behind them. Water dripped from the ceiling, stood in pools and ran in little streams. The hunters hung back, looking anxiously around as pictures appeared ahead and crawled slowly behind them on the walls. Reaching a marrowbone hole that led upward, she found a foothold and started to climb. Scratcher spoke from below.

"I never came this deep in."

Instantly the others stopped, murmuring among themselves. Drogben, who had fought a cave lion, who once fought half the Wolf-Kill band and escaped with his life, even Drogben trembled here. Because they had praised her picture, Nyori felt strong. She looked down on them, Anzeel standing far behind the others. Now, it seemed, he wouldn't come near her.

"Deep is powerful," she told them, beginning to learn the craft of lying.

Up through the marrowbone, she led them at last to the low chamber where, coming through the hill the other direction with Anzeel and Otti, she had found the good clay. The little bison figure she'd made was still there—crudely scuptured. She could do better now.

Nyori broke off one of the sharp stone teeth-that-grow and dug the point into the floor, scoring a bison outline deeply into the clay. This time she cut in behind it to remove a slab. She cut a second slab . Rothgar carried the first, she the second, staggering under the weight into a round chamber barely high enough for the men to dance.

"Statues?" Scratcher said.

"Yes."

The old man seemed both impressed and doubtful. She and Rothgar had just placed the slabs against a boulder that stuck up from the floor when Scratcher began his barefoot dance, chanting:

"BI-son, BI-son, BI-son, BI-son," then changing, "bi-SON, bi-SON, bi-SON, bi-SON..." Other voices took it up, as did the cave itself, answering deep voiced and hollow: "SON...OON...OON" The hunters circled Nyori, lifting their feet as if stalking through high grass, throwing hands up to shade their eyes in searching for a herd.

She knelt before the fresh clay, struggling to think amid this noise. Studying the rough boulder, the way it jutted from the cave floor, Nyori let her mind go blank. She looked at the boulder and the two clay slabs. Then she closed her eyes and saw them: a cow bison and a bull pausing on a hilltop beside an up-thrusting, out-thrusting crag of rock.

"BI-son, BI-son, BI-son...."

She slid the slabs back and forth until their positions matched her vision, then fixed them in place with handfuls of wet clay. She sliced with her flint to rough-shape the outlines of bull and cow. These statues would be bigger than anything Nyori had ever carved in bone, yet in clay they were easy and quick.

The dancers squatted low to earth, jumped high and pranced around her. Their dance told how, at the World's beginning, Irta had created Bison to be both friends with the Steppe People and food for their bellies. Listening to the patter of many feet, Nyori worked a long time before the chant suddenly changed.

"Bison START, bison START, bison START..."

Jerkily, Sudrog pounded one bone on another, making a sound truer than the figures she was shaping—hollow hoofbeats of bison as they turned now this way, now that, searching for the source of danger.

"START...ART...ART..." returned the voice of Deep Earth.

Anzeel was farthest out in the circle, farthest from Nyori. Biting his lip between white teeth, squeezing his eyes tight shut, he danced wildest of them all and still played his bone flute. It twittered like the bird flocks that followed the herds. Anzeel believed so deeply that he should have been the scratcher. But it was she, Nyori, who now shaped the figures.

One dancer still carried a lamp. Others had placed them around the chamber. First light, then shadow, fell across her hands as she molded shoulder humps with fingertips, clay squeezing tight under her nails. She rolled little points between her palms and smoothed them into the heads for horns. Other rolls of clay became arched bison tails.

"Bison RUN, bison RUN, bison RUN..."

Sudrog's bones pounded swifter as the herd swirled, alarmed, and raced away from the hunters.

"RUN...UN...UN..." Deep Earth sang back.

Sweating, shining dancers whirled and turned, Scratcher throwing his reindeer-horned head about, flaunting the horse tail of his costume, not even noticing that his funny old sex parts dangled out through a hole in the seat of his leather trousers.

"Bison FALL, bison FALL, bison FALL..."

The dancers threw themselves high, leaping, groaning, crashing to earth.

"FALL...ALL...ALL..."

With the sharp edge of her flint, Nyori finished by slashing quick lines for the animals' manes and dewlap bristles. She knew the figures were hurriedly, coarsely shaped, not so fine as the bison she had carved in antler. But with the herd's thunder in her ears, she sat back to look at the statues, lamplight still blazing and dimming across their clay flesh as they stood tensely on the rocky crag. And she had sighed out her satisfaction with her work of that night.

Now, trudging up this endless hill in a line of empty-bellied hunters, she wondered what failure it all would bring, what would happen after.

Not that it wasn't time for bison. Even if snow had come, the sun was far advanced in its seasonal passage, already well up from the Warm Sky horizon. The animals were late.

As they walked, the Land leveled before them, then tilted down toward the creek that crossed the slope. Ahead, where water glittered between tree trunks, there came a twittering of birds, and she thought of Anzeel's flute. A flock burst up through greening branches and flew toward Nyori and Scratcher, wings beating in flurries, then pausing as the birds hurtled like gray stones through the air, then beating furiously again. A flight of doves, which whistled above Nyori's head and away across the prairie beyond. Scratcher's hand came out to stop her.

"What scared the doves?" he whispered.

The old man ghosted ahead of her down toward the creek, angling to the left. Nyori followed, threading her way through prickly raspberry canes that held no fruit. She caught up at the water. Amid a welter of bird tracks in the mud, Scratcher stood beside a flat pile of dung, steaming in the cool air. Big cloven hoof prints crossed the creek here and turned to the left, many lines of hooves, water still flowing into those squished in mud at the edge. The little breeze that blew on her face was dark and rich with animal odor. Nyori felt herself tremble, heard the breath in her throat. They backed out of the creek bed, getting far enough away so they dared say more in whispers.

"Bison moving left," he said, "away from our hunting line. I can't keep up, Nyori. Wind is good. They won't smell you. Now run, stay this side of the creek so they won't hear, run far ahead and turn them back."

"What if they don't turn?"

"Yell. Break off a branch and wave it."

Nyori ran. She carried the lance in her left hand, held well forward so the point would not stab her if she fell. She grabbed at a pine tree, snapping off a needled branch. She ran on through grass, the creek bed with its tall trees on her right. Bramble patches thickened on the slope ahead. She had to pick her way slowly through them. A grunting, grumbling, rumbling, drifted to her from brush on her right. Bison! Bison murmuring among themselves. Nyori angled away from them so they wouldn't hear and once more ran.

Trees on the far side of the creek opened out into a little

clearing. No bison were crossing it. She was ahead! She tried to cross the creek on stones but fell in, wetting her sandals. She had barely splashed up onto the far bank when tree branches shook and an old bison cow ambled out. A bull followed her, then a dozen more—three calves and a bunch of yearlings. Nyori stood ahead of them, a little on the creek side. She didn't want them to escape across it.

"Ho, bison!" she called. "Go back!"

She jumped high to make herself tall. She waved the pine tree branch. The herd ambled slowly toward her. They must know she was one of those fearful humans with their lances and clubs. Still the bison came on.

"Whoa! Whoa! Go back!"

The others stopped, but the cow and bull kept on, breathing steam from their nostrils. Nyori dare not run. The Horse Band had to get meat, *had* to. Holding the branch with her left hand, she cocked her lance in the other as if about to throw.

"I'll kill you!" she screamed. "I will!"

As if embarrassed, the old cow paused and turned her head aside, looking down toward the creek. Then she came on. The earth was packed, not muddy here at all. Yet when bison hooves came down on it, they cut deep prints.

"You die, bison! Turn now, or you die!" She tried to sound like Torfinn.

Violently, she waved the pine branch in their faces. The bull, with his huge hump, moved ahead of the cow, staring at the branch as if he wanted to eat it. Then he stopped, so close she could touch him with her lance—not that she wanted to touch him, oh no! So close she saw the gray-sprinkled swirl of hair centered in his broad brow, like the swirl on top of Anzeel's head. The bull snorted nostril steam out toward her legs. An eddy in the breeze brought her his odor, a blurry blend of sweat and dung, strangely pleasant to this child of a hunting band. The bison towered above her, his ragged, shedding springtime hide rippling as it shook off itches. She stared into brown eyes as big as her own clenched fists.

"Bison, go back! Please go! Please!"

The bull turned a little to his right and dropped his head as if about to graze, but there was no grass. With her mild, bored eyes, the cow still looked at Nyori.

"Please, please, please!"

The cow turned behind the bull, and the others followed up from the creek, heading where Nyori wanted them to go, back toward the line of hunters.

"Thank you, bison!"

But there was more to getting meat than turning the game. She followed the herd out of the woods, up onto the prairie slope beyond. The wet grass stuffed into her sandals for warmth squished with every step. Scratcher came out of trees to her right, his deep voice sounding.

"Bison START, Bison START..."

Other hunters, spread far beyond him across the slope, glanced this way and took up the chant. The cow broke into a trot, the rest of the herd following. Nyori ran to keep up. She had to stay close, had to shoo the bison across the line of hunters. Scratcher limped forward far too slowly but threw anyway, his lance falling short. The herd angled more steeply up the hill and whirled away from him, hooves ripping the ground, throwing up chunks of sod as they broke into a gallop.

"Bison RUN, Bison RUN..."

Nyori fell down in a tangle of briers. She rose with bleeding legs and ran on. As bison crossed ahead of them, hunters rushed forward one by one to cast their lances. Nyori saw a lance point bounce off the bull's flank. Another stuck for an instant in a yearling's hide, then fell out as the animal spurted ahead. Most of the lances fell short. The men couldn't keep up with that shambling gallop. Where were the band's fastest runners—Drogben and Anzeel? Nowhere to be seen just when they were needed most. The bison were escaping, racing up toward the hilltop where an up-thrusting, out-thrusting crag of rock stood against blank gray sky.

Suddenly two figures rose from snow ahead of the herd, two bodies as white from the waist up as snow itself. It was Drogben and Anzeel! Though closer than anyone to the game, they did not cock their lances for throwing. They had stripped off their hide tops and now held the sleeves, furiously waving the garments, the shell-decorated tunic flapping wildly. Recoiling from Drogben and Anzeel, most of the herd shied to the left and vanished across the hilltop to the other side. The bull and cow swerved right and stopped, kicking up a shower of gravel.

Their great sides heaved as they panted, snorting gouts of steam, which swirled away on the breeze. They stood just short of the rocky crag, separated a little but still together, as if they had been together a long time. Nyori's eyes sucked them in, she feeling deep in her brain this tingle of recognition: it was her sculpture, the magic sculpture she had made in Deep Earth.

The cow and bull held there a moment, as if to catch their breath, then they too swung left and disappeared across the hilltop to the other side. Drogben and Anzeel didn't move. Why hadn't they hurled their lances? Why didn't they chase? Nyori ran after the bison. They must not get away! She saw Anzeel running too but in the wrong direction.

"Not at me!" she screamed. "Chase the bison!"

He collided with her at the hill crest. They fell in a tangle of arms and legs. His shock of hair shut out the light, the cold skin of his upper body smelling of wood smoke and outdoor air.

"You dung beetle!" she yelled. "You cockroach, you let them get away!"

With hands on her shoulders, he lifted her to sitting position, then rose and moved off. Furious, Nyori jumped up, scrabbling on stones that rolled under her feet.

Only then did she see that this hill had no other side—just a straight-down cliff. The round stones bounced to its edge and fell cleanly through the air. She took hold of a little shrub and leaned out so her eyes could follow. Far below where the stones pattered down, lay a scattering of brown bodies. Here and there a raised leg with its black hoof still kicked. Bright blood splashed the snow around them.

She felt sorry for the bison, most of all for the cow and bull, yet she couldn't fight back the smile that crept out on her cheeks. Again she felt that triumphant surge of blood in her brain. Her magic had led the herd to its death and would feed the Horse Band.

Now she wanted to believe. It was her magic. *Hers*.

10

Comfortless

From the butchering ground, they carried her home to Owl Cave, never allowing her feet to touch the ground. First Drogben, then Rothgar, then Sudrog carried her high on their shoulders.

Not Anzeel. He was too little anyhow, but he kept far away from Nyori. She held Sudrog's stiff curls to steady herself, riding him as god Irta might have ridden her hairy mammoth. From that high perch she let her eyes blaze on Anzeel's averted face. If he was still jealous of her scratching, well, that was just fine!

Others carried bison haunches on their shoulders, or two men together dragged the gutted carcass of a yearling. They spread bison hides on the ground and loaded them with the best cuts of meat to be dragged home. They took only what they could haul in one trip, leaving the rest for hyenas and the tawny cave lion that watched the butchering from a high place in the rocks. Since Wolf-Kill territory was close by, they dare not return for more.

From afar through the dimming light of dusk, Horse Band women saw the hunters coming, ran to meet them, danced and yelled as they brought the meat in. Sudrog lifted Nyori high from his shoulders and set her down before Anzeel's mother, who dropped her eyes to the cave floor and stood there trembling.

"Kansi?" Nyori said.

She wanted to be hugged by her foster-mother, wanted her feet lifted from the ground, wanted kisses on her cheeks. But Kansi was suddenly shy. So were the other women, and the men as well. Men who had told jokes on Scratcher, who ridiculed him for his failures, were afraid even to look full into Nyori's eyes after her success. Uneasy at first, she began to like this strange homage.

That night they built fires and cooked a feast. Kansi roasted delicate strips of liver and carried them to Nyori on a sharpened stick. She sat near the cave entrance, sat there like a ruler, like Scratcher in the old days, chewing the smoky meat as blood ran from the corners of her mouth.

Next day the sun shone brightly on melting snow. Using sharpened bison shoulder blades to dig, the Horse People widened an old hole outside the cave, making it waist deep on the digger, wide as the span of her arms. They used a scraped bison hide to line the hole, then filled it with snow. Heating stones in the fire, they dropped them in to make snow melt, added more snow, then more hot stones. Soon the water roiled and bubbled and steamed.

By then the sun had changed rolling hills of the Land from winter white back to the green and brown of spring. The people carried hide sacks of acorns from the woods, along with oak galls and bark, and dumped them into the water. This bled bitterness from the oak stuff, after which the acorns were gathered from the water. The Horse People roasted acorns over the fire, shelled and ate them.

Nyori got the best ones, enjoying their mealiness on her tongue, sweetening as she chewed. They were deliciously different from meat. Into the cooling, bitter water—still thick with oak galls and bark—went the bison hides, which would soak three days while the bitterness changed rawhide to leather.

Anzeel and Riba worked together on this, punching hides down in the water, turning them, laughing and talking all the while. Riba was a round-hipped woman, heavy bosomed—too old for Anzeel. Still, she looked hungrily at his slim chest, more beautiful for the seashell pattern Nyori had sewn on his tunic. Nyori saw him stare openly back at Riba.

When he next walked past, Nyori called:

"Anzeel!"

He stopped and stood looking not quite at her, his lips twisted bitterly—as if he'd tasted water from the hole.

"Those are my shells," she told him, "those decorations on your tunic. I bored holes in the shells to take split sinew. I sewed them on. It's your tunic, but they're my shells."

A cook fire burns smoky orange on top, yet the hottest flame flickers blue white near the coals. Anzeel's eyes shone with that same pale fire as he turned, staring directly into her as no one else had dared since her success. He shrugged upward with his arms, shrugged upward again, sliding the tunic over his head, until he stood snowy chested before her. He plopped the tunic at her feet, turned and ducked into the low cave opening.

"You come back! Anzeel!"

He did not come back. Still turning the hides, Riba watched slyly from the corner of her eye. Nyori saw others watching. She shrugged her own shoulders upward, shrugged again, sliding out of her tunic like a snake from its weary skin. The air chilled her chest. She looked down at the two swellings, hardly bigger than Anzeel's, which promised she might one day be like Riba. The whiteness was stippled with gooseflesh, the brown nipples shrunken. She raised Anzeel's tunic high and let it slide down over her arms, over her body. This was the tunic, the very one, that had shied the bison off the cliff. It was warm inside, still warm from Anzeel. She hugged it close around her and tried to breathe the air.

This was only right, that the Horse Band's Scratcher should have a shell-decorated tunic. More important, much more, she had become what she wanted to be—the Horse Band's Scratcher Woman. Why, then, did her eyes sting so badly that she had to walk blindly away from the workers, staring out across the Land as she pretended to search for a second herd that might be called up by her magic.

Over the lengthening days of the next moon, two herds did fall victim, one of horse, another of reindeer. Each time she scratched her picture, the hunters danced and the herd appeared. Maybe it is magic. Maybe *I'm* magic, Nyori thought. But the belief that had filled her as she stood on the bison-kill cliff, that never quite returned.

With more meat than they could use, the people sliced long strips to dry over a smoky fire, fatty marrow-filled bones of bison and horse burning in the fire, making the smoke that preserved their own flesh. It was a busy time. The women made needles, cutting two deep grooves side by side on a horse thigh bone, then prying out the long splinter between, which could be shaped and polished and drilled with a stone awl to take threads of split sinew. With bison leather ready, everyone worked on new garments, cutting and sewing.

Soon after their quarrel over the shell-decorated tunic, Scratcher Woman had seen Anzeel shivering within a bison robe he had pulled around his bare upper body. She threw him her old plain tunic. She was glad when he put it on, glad when he hugged hers close about him, as she had hugged his. When leather from the first hunt was ready, though, his mother helped him sew a new tunic for himself.

Nyori returned one night to find her plain tunic laid out on her bed. She slid her hand inside and discovered the worn leather was cold and comfortless. She lay down beside her sleeping little brother, stroked the smooth skin of his forehead, his round cheeks, felt his breath blow warm on her hand. It was nearly dawn before she went to sleep.

Out of famine, the Horse Band had fallen into plenty, which was their usual state of life. The Land was wide and often generous. Once more the people had plenty to eat, plenty to put on, plenty of time to make weapons and tools and ornaments, time to play games. They had more time for quarrels among themselves. Still, most were happy.

Not Lee-Tan and Torfinn. Ever since Torfinn's defeat, those two had skulked around the cave, muttering about the Evil and Nyori. Approaching her, they would throw up hands to shield themselves from her glance—deadlier, they pretended, than the flight of Drogben's lance.

Awakening one morning, Nyori found Scratcher sitting cross-legged in the dust beside her bed. He said nothing and hardly needed to. As he groped a hand out to find hers, Nyori saw trouble in his face.

"Torfinn's gone," Scratcher said. "Lee-Tan too. They took all the tanned leather they could carry and left."

Nyori sighed happily.

"We don't need them."

Her remark did nothing to banish gloom from Scratcher's face.

75

"Drogben followed their trail as far as Rocky Ledge, then lost them. Where did they go?"

"Back toward sunrise sky? Back to People of the Steppe?"

"I hope so," Scratcher said.

"Where else could they go? *Who* else could they go to?"

He didn't answer, except with a shrug.

11

I *Know* You

Nyori had full freedom now in Deep Earth. She studied pictures by the Ancients and made any picture she liked. Old Scratcher even showed her how to put light in the eyes of her creatures, as he had with his cave lion.

"I'm good with parts," he told her. "Not good anymore with the whole."

She wanted to do more than scratch, however. She wanted to try painting at least part of a picture. She asked the old man for ocher, a fine earth which, when burned, changed to a rich yellow or brown, sometimes red. He gave her a handful. She mixed it with melted fat in the bowl of her sandstone lamp, making a thin paint the color of old blood. Scratcher showed her how to split the end of a willow twig, split it countless times into a brush with fibers fine as horse hair.

Because the paint dish had to be held constantly level, she would need help—someone taller and steadier than Otti, who usually got bored with her scratching and fell asleep. She found Kansi, who was sewing the long seam of a trouser leg.

"Kansi, come," she said.

Kansi rose slowly and followed right to the Deep Earth Arch, where she stopped.

"Not to Deep Earth." She shook her head and backed away.

"I'm Scratcher Woman. Kansi, come!.."

Grabbing her hands, Nyori tugged her toward the arch. Kansi was a big woman. When she set her feet, Nyori couldn't budge her. Others watched, Anzeel sitting far from his mother's place, sitting with that hussy Riba.

"Kansi, I need you!" Nyori shouted. She yanked at the hands.

"I'm afraid. Irta...Irta....." She turned the god's name into an agonized groan. "No women in Deep Earth!"

"I'm a woman. If I can do it, you can."

"But you're the child of Irta."

They believed what Scratcher told them. Scratcher stepped between Kansi and Nyori.

"Don't force her."

Nyori was surprised that the old man would oppose her. It was he, after all, who'd made her Scratcher Woman. She felt the snort of indignant breath through her own nostrils but let the hands slip free. Kansi fled back to her fire. The old man's eyes roved the cave until they settled on Riba's nook.

"Anzeel! Go with Scratcher Woman. Help her."

He rose from beside Riba, moved grudgingly, as if he hated to leave. Holding a borrowed oil lamp, Nyori led the way through the Arch with Otti close behind. Anzeel—the stubborn fool—hung back, stumbling often because he was so far from the light. She walked deliberately fast and directly to the Womb Shrine.

There she chose the place on the wall above her Bawling Bison. It was the highest wall in the Shrine, yet no Ancient had made a picture there, perhaps because light from an oil lamp held at head level hardly reached it. Nyori crawled up a ledge, rested her right foot on a projecting rock, half turned and managed to brace her back against a second ledge, hanging there twice man-height above the floor. Anzeel handed up her pouch with scratching flints and the brush.

"You could talk to me," she said.

He didn't reply but then, seeing that his lamp didn't shine on the rock face, he inched upward on a ledge to bring it closer. In its wavering light she studied bare gray curves of stone close to her face. What picture would she make? The band had plenty of meat, no need to call the dancers and scratch an animal. So, what picture? As water had boiled in the hole, something boiled now inside her. It was the nearness of Anzeel. She wanted to shock him, make him feel as she felt.

Then she saw it in her mind: Scratcher in his reindeer costume, old Scratcher leading the dance around her bison sculptures in Deep Earth. She took out her flint burin and, as had become usual with her, first cut the long curved line of the figure's back, rising at his rump, sweeping over to his legs. The moving shadow of her arm made it hard to see the flint.

The old man's upper body was skinny, but he still had powerful legs. She started sketching them in, her burin flint biting at the stone. Dancing, he moved to her left, turning his head to look inward at her. She scratched the forward line of the left leg, knee bent, then carried it down to the foot and made toes, only four, because the bear had bitten one off.

"That's a man foot!" Anzeel exclaimed. "Scratcher's foot!"

She said nothing, just cut in the graceful horse tail of his costume. She lay a hand across her lips and felt a smile grow under it. Anzeel's voice came up to her then, more solemn than angry.

"Remember Irta," he said, repeating the old words, "remember, Deep Earth is her womb, everything is born of it. Whatever we scratch on the walls, those things appear on the prairie above, on the tundra, in the forest when reindeer and bison and horses drop their young. Nyori, you don't know what this might do to Scratcher."

To satisfy him, she shaped the figure's head less like Scratcher's, more like a reindeer head with upthrust hairy ears and tall branching horns. But out of the reindeer mask stared the eyes of Scratcher, wide, haunted eyes struggling to see through the white fog that was blinding him.

"If you really believed," Anzeel said, "you wouldn't make a picture of Scratcher. You wouldn't capture his soul on the wall."

She turned to look down at him. The lamp cast its brightest light on his sober, upturned face.

"I love Scratcher," she said.

"That's what I mean. You wouldn't do that to him. Ever since we ran the bison off the cliff, you pretend. But you don't believe in Irta."

She wanted to believe, now at least she wanted to. She gestured to the picture.

"If this is bad, why doesn't it scare you? If you believe, why don't you run away, why don't you bow down to me like the rest of them?"

"Because I *know* you," he said.

It was neither praise nor insult. It was only his words, yet she felt a quickening of blood around her heart.

"Because I'm a woman, that's the reason, isn't it? But you believe in a woman god. You believe in Irta."

"That's different."

"Different because you never saw Irta. People told you about her. But you *know* me."

"Isn't that just what I said?"

"You know Scratcher too. Why did you believe in him?"

"I don't believe in anybody now. No person."

"If you don't believe," she yelled at him, "then why don't you quit arguing about *my* belief. Can't you leave me alone about that?"

She said it so loudly that the cave sang back, "A-LONE...LONE..."

Otti had been sitting in dust on the cave floor below them. Now his head jerked up and he stared at them.

"I do believe in Irta. But, yes, I'll leave you alone!" Anzeel yelled, and still he didn't leave. "What's wrong with you?" he shouted. "I brought everyone here to see your great bison picture. You said I told on you. *Told on you*, as if I tried to hurt you. You don't believe, and still you bully everybody. You tried to drag my mother in here. You tried to force her. You eat the best meat. You let people wait on you."

"Well, I'm Scratcher Woman!"

"You're nothing like our old Scratcher."

"Would you be a better one?"

"I would if you taught me how!"

Their voices roared around them, sounding back and forth through the cave. When the echoes died, she heard her brother wailing. He sat with both hands raised to cover his ears.

"Stop fight!" he groaned. "Please, please..."

"You're making Otti cry," Nyori said.

"It's not me, it's you," he said, and then looked away from her. After a moment, he sighed. "Go ahead, finish it, whatever it's supposed to be."

She steadied herself on the ledge and took long breaths to calm herself.

"Hand up the paint." With the willow twig brush, she painted broad strokes of ocher on Scratcher's legs, almost as if she were shaping the muscles under his skin. With quick sweeps, she strengthened the lines of his back and chest and shoulders under the reindeer hide costume. Finished, she climbed halfway down from the ceiling to Anzeel's ledge and took the lamp, holding it high to see Scratcher dancing.

"That will scare people to death," Anzeel told her.

"They won't see it up here in the dark."

This didn't mollify him. He stood beside on her the ledge, his brow furrowed, that blue heat shining from his eyes.

"Nyori, all you ever think about is scratching. You don't care about people anymore. You don't care about me."

She thought of the lance that bounced off the bison's hide, wishing her tunic of bison leather could as easily turn his words.

"If I'm so bad," she said, "if you hate me so much, why did you save my life on the cliff? You stopped me from running off behind the herd. That's the second time you saved me."

"You noticed!" he snorted. "I'm surprised. I didn't think you noticed anything except yourself."

They were not shouting now. Still, Otti's voice wailed from below.

"No fight!"

Anzeel turned away from her, jumped down from their perch and started back toward the cave entrance. He passed the water-dripping ledge and disappeared in utter blackness.

"Wait!" she called. "Wait for the lamp."

She heard him bumping into things, heard him fall down and scramble up and fall again, before the sounds died away. When he came out at the entrance, he would have bruises on his shoulders, knots on his head, which he would well deserve. He was barely out of hearing when Nyori found herself struggling to remember one thing he had said, one thing she had not answered. What was it?

I would if you taught me how!

He would be a better Scratcher, better than Nyori, if she taught him. Well, the way he was acting, she wouldn't. She wouldn't teach him anything. She stood there trembling on her perch. He's so dumb, she thought. She was trying to stay mad at him because he was mad at her, at the same time feeling her lips shape soundless, despairing words: Will this never end? Will it never never end?

12

Not for My Mother!

After that she felt ashamed when people served her, but they insisted. They seemed to want it. She let it happen. They wanted her to scratch, and she let that happen too. She made pictures in Deep Earth, all the while thinking over how she had become what Anzeel described: a Scratcher Woman who thought of nothing except herself and scratching.

Spring was on them now, warm and sweet, the Land blooming green beyond the cave entrance. One day she saw Scratcher take up a fish spear and walk out into it. She wanted release. As he started down the hill toward the creek, she ran to catch him.

"Can you see well enough to spear salmon?" she asked.

"No."

Then why was he going? After a long walk, they came around the hill, down to the river at a deep pool, its glossy skin of water wrinkled only where salmon fins reached up to brush the surface.

"Never catch fish here," Scratcher sighed. "Need a narrow place."

Through leafy willow thickets, past shiny-petaled flowers blooming yellow against brown mud, he led her down to where the pool thinned itself to nearly nothing. It broke across a rock ledge there and roared into rapids below. Sunlight blazed on the foam, making her blink. Scratcher untied his sandals and kicked them off. She did the same. Together they waded into the stream, Nyori gasping at the icy bite of water on her feet. She held his arm to steady him. Then, as her feet skidded on the slime, felt *him* support her—an old man sturdy as a rooted oak.

Beside a gravel bar near the far shore, they found the one reach where current sucked itself down into a sharp V. Here the water was thigh deep, the only place salmon could swim up the rapid. The instant her foot searched for bottom, she felt something slick bump her ankle, something solid. Water around her legs throbbed with dark shapes, pumping hard with their tails but still only crawling against that current. Scratcher stared blindly down into the river, looking bewildered.

"Salmon!" she shouted over the roar. "Can you see them?"

"No."

"How can you spear them?"

Scratcher threw his fish spear butt first out onto the gravel bar. Then he bent to thrust his arms shoulder deep in the stream, one ear dipping as he turned his head aside to breathe. Nyori watched him blink thoughtfully and bite his tongue between stained front teeth. His shoulders twitched as his two hands searched the depths between his legs.

"Whooo-o-o-o-ops!" he yelled.

His body jerked upward, arms flying behind it, the hands just balancing a salmon half as long as Nyori. It flew high, flopping, and arched out onto the gravel bar. There it bounced up and fell back, scattering twigs of driftwood with its violence, bounced up again and yet again—getting no closer to the water that was its home.

"Big mama fish," Scratcher announced. "Full of eggs."

"How did you do it?"

"Feel up along her flank, pet her a little bit. She'll like it. Slowly bring in a hand on each side about the middle and pet her there. Then throw her out on the bar."

On her first try she got the salmon only half out before it tilted forward off her hands and shot upstream. She didn't have the strength to throw it clear out. Again she bent until her nose brushed cold water, staring down at the red rocks of the bottom. A big male, its hooked upper jaw overhanging the lower, swam idly behind her right thigh, sheltering himself from current in the eddy there.

Nyori reached back between her legs and touched the pink belly. Uneasy, the fish moved out into current and swam forward, right between two human hands that ached with cold. Nyori tickled his sides as the salmon came through, and he hesitated. Aaaaaaaah, that felt good, that tickling. This time she wouldn't try the throw. Instead, she edged caressing fingers forward, slowly forward on both sides, almost into the wildly-pumping gills.

"Ya!" she yelled, jamming fingers full into the gills and lifting straight up. The fish rose from the water, thumping her with his muscular body. She pushed hands through from both sides until fingers locked in the middle. She wouldn't let go. No! A fountain of spray rose as the fish flailed her. His big mouth gaped level with hers while his tail pounded her thighs and bottom. Through exploding spray, she caught a glimpse of Scratcher's grin before a thudding blow knocked her feet sideways on the slime.

"Yi-i-i-i!"

She saw blue sky and then the same blueness through water, bubbles from her own breath rising. She felt herself lifted, carried headlong downstream. She rolled through the fast water, banging rocks, sliding over logs, ducking under branches. Finally she got her head high enough to gulp in air, as she did on the day long ago when she swam into Deep Earth.

"Ah-a-a-a-a-a-a!"

The salmon plunged against the grip of her hands, hammered her with his tail. She fought him and the water until, at last, current spit her out into a quiet pool at the bottom. She stood up shakily and lifted the exhausted fish, held it high so Scratcher could see. Of course, he couldn't. From his stance far away at the head of the rapid, he squinted at her and said:

"You hurt?"

"I got him!" she yelled.

Between them, they threw out seven more big salmon. They cut gills from the fish and gutted them, leaving yellow clusters of eggs in the females. Scratcher tied the salmon up in a line along his stout fish spear. That's how they would carry them home, he holding one end of the shaft, she the other. But by then Nyori—her shell-decorated tunic dripping with water, her wrinkled hands bluish with cold—was shivering deep inside. Nearly-blind old Scratcher sensed it. He touched her icy arm with a hand that seemed hot, saying:

"Start a fire. We eat fish before we go back."

The old man carried his own firestone and flint. He pulled handfuls of dry grass for tinder and knelt over it, making showers of sparks.

"This I can still do," he murmured.

Starting the fire, he had to keep turning his head, trying to see through little openings that still remained in his eye-clouds. From Nyori's big male, they cut boneless strips of pink flesh, which she roasted on forked branches, working close to the fire. Soon her leather garments steamed in the breeze.

They blew on the strips to cool them, then ate hungrily, hardly chewing the juicy meat with its rich smoke flavors. When it was gone, they licked fingers clean and sat there, stuffed but somehow still not satisfied. Nyori's eye roved the marshy bank, fixing on a patch of slim leaves.

"Cattails!"

She ran to them, bunched leaves together in her hands and yanked the plants up from mud. She carried many roots back to the fire. Washed in river water, peeled with a flint blade, the raw tubers crunched delightfully between her teeth, tasting sweetly of the earth. Scratcher chewed and swallowed big mouthfuls.

As the sun settled toward pink mists at the horizon, she ate her last bite and sat there, at last both belly-full and belly-happy. With that hunger satisfied, another took its place. She wanted an answer to Anzeel's question: how had she become what she was?

Scratcher lay back on the gravel, his dimming eyes turned skyward. So far only the brightest stars had burned through, winking against that paleness. He clasped hands behind his head, cradling it. The gesture tugged his tunic sleeves upward and bared his forearms. They were thick with scars, dull-red dots where single teeth had penetrated, rope-like masses of twisted skin where the huge mouth had chewed his flesh.

"Scratcher, tell me about the bear."

"We have to carry fish home," he said. "Be dark soon. You got to lead me."

"I'll lead you. *Tell* it."

He sat up, groaning, and leaned forward to hug his bent knees with the scarred arms.

"Nyori, I wanted to *rest*." But he started telling it anyway, how they had returned to Owl Cave that spring when Nyori was six winters old. Inside the first chamber, they found themselves facing a bear just awakened from his long sleep.

"He was sluggish, you know. Torfinn was up front with me, he thought it would be easy. The bear didn't want to fight, he ran back in that nook—you know, where I whipped you that day." At his recollection of the punishment he'd laid on the children, the old man smiled, as did Nyori.

"We lighted torches and followed the bear. Anupa, your mother, she left you outside with Kansi. She followed us and tried to make me stop. We didn't need meat. She told me to get out of the way, let the bear leave the cave. I was just stupid. Anupa..." he said and then fell silent. Scratcher stared gloomily into the fire, eyes liquid and unfocused, pink with light from the horizon.

"What were you going to say about my mother?" she asked.

"I don't know." The old man shrugged. "When we came into that nook, I smelled the bear, real strong. He kept growling, trying to warn us away, but I was stupid. Then everything got quiet. He hid and waited till we passed him, then came roaring out. I drove my lance into his chest. I stabbed him in the shoulders, stabbed him in the neck. He knocked me backwards."

Scratcher hugged his knees tighter to his chest, rocking back and forth on the gravel of the bar. The breath hissed out of him in a long sigh.

"This is *hard* on me, telling it."

"I know." Nyori felt a thickness in her own chest.

"Well," Scratcher said, "well, Torfinn didn't help, he ran back out into daylight. The bear clawed me all over. He bit my arms and shoulders. I smelled that awful breath. I saw blood spurt, must be my blood, I thought, but felt nothing. It didn't hurt. Like a dream I couldn't wake up from. Many times I dream it since then."

Nyori's own breath was coming quickly now, as if she were part of the fight.

"Where was my mother?"

The old man's mouth widened in a smile.

"She was there, but off to one side. By Irta, your mother was strong! My torch was still burning up on a ledge. That's how I saw her. She yanked my lance out of the bear's neck and stuck him in the chest. She yanked it out and hit him again. I saw her lean hard on that shaft, reaching for his heart. The bear was like me, he wasn't feeling anything. He was so busy killing me he didn't notice Anupa was killing him. Finally he swung on her, knocked her down. He bit her once on the leg, but she didn't quit stabbing.

"It was more than the bear could stand. He let her go and limped deeper into the nook. That's where they found him dead."

"I know where you found him," she said, "because I came in there with Kansi. I saw him dead."

"He wasn't a bad bear, Nyori. It wasn't the bear's fault."

When Scratcher fell silent, they heard night sounds rising around them, the creaking of frogs beside the river, the distant bark of a jackal.

"What happened to my mother?"

Scratcher sat there like a burned-out old stump. He said:

"They made a fuss about me because I got chewed all over, I was bleeding. Anupa cleaned my cuts, fed me, took care. My wounds started healing and hers didn't. Her leg swelled up, turned red around that bite. Red like salmon meat, it crawled down to her ankle and up to her thigh..." He trailed off and stopped talking. Nyori lay the fingers of one hand on the scars of his wrist.

"Tell me about you and my mother."

"You know."

"Tell it again."

Scratcher threw his arms out.

"Will you never let me rest!" Then, low voiced, he took it up again. "Well, she liked me, Anupa did. Her man had died. He was your father, but you never knew him. My woman had died before. I was too old for your mother, but we liked each other. We were man and woman together two winters. Then that bear. I got hurt, she got bitten. I tried to save her, Nyori. I danced and prayed to Irta..."

She had wanted it, she had asked for the story. Now she felt sudden heat around her heart, a flaming impatience.

"If Irta doesn't help you, if Irta let my mother die, why do you believe in her?"

The old man shrugged, opening his hands to the sky.

"Sometimes she helps."

"*Some*times!" Nyori shouted at him. "But not for my mother!"

"She helps the Horse Band.   Sometimes she does. She's Great Mother. We come from her. Because we know this, we care for one another in the band."

"And hate everybody outside? That's what the Wolf-Kills do. *Their* Irta makes them hate everybody else."

"In the Horse Band we're not so bad."

His very calmness made her angry.

"*Sometimes*," she yelled, "but not for my mother!"

Scratcher hugged his knees again, staring into the coals of the fire. Far away the jackal howled, faint on the night, this time answered by an even more distant stutter of yips and yowls. Scratcher raised his pinched face to the stars, opened his mouth and mourned in a voice pitched higher than the jackals'.

"Ay-ye-ye-ye-ye!" he mourned. "Ay-yeeeeee...!"

Reminded of it all, she now hated Irta more than she hated the bear. No, she did not believe, she would not believe in the god who let her mother die. Since she didn't know how the god might look, it was the bear she decided to create.   This time she went alone to the Womb Shrine, choosing a place easier to reach, far below her own picture of Scratcher dancing in reindeer costume. She set her oil lamp on a ledge and squeezed pebbles under one end to steady it. Lamp light danced brightly on the nearest wall.

She herself had seen the bloody heap, all that was left of the bear that killed her mother. Here she would make her own bear, here under her own picture of Scratcher, which—though Scratcher himself might die—forevermore would hold dominion over the bear.

She would scratch the animal as she remembered him, lying on his right side, bleeding his life out in the dirt. This would not be like her earlier pictures, she would not draw with careful thought. No. She took out her sharpest burin, testing it with her thumb, jabbing so her own flesh bled before the bear's.

Then she stood up to the stone and attacked it. The flint point cut deep as she yanked the burin along, scattering chips which tinkled down across the rock face to the floor. First she slashed the line of the bear's back, letting the point rise up over the shoulder hump before she pulled it down, around the curve of hips. She cut the jagged triangle of the ear, then the skull's dome on both sides, sliding into the blunt snout. She pulled one front leg straight down, the paw flattened, extended and relaxed, because this animal was dead. He was dead. Atop those feet she raked deep grooves, meant to be the bear's own claws but really more like the scars on Scratcher's face.

Next came the right front leg, cut in behind the left, and then the belly—a row of sharp, vertical cuts to show his winter fur. Finally, a wavy slash downward, rightward to put in the last line of the hind legs. So the outline was finished. She saw it was truly the bear that killed her mother.

Her mother. Had Nyori only dreamed her? No, she remembered a few things. How, when Nyori was old enough to realize the strangeness, she saw another woman feeding a new baby. She asked her own mother about it and was told that she, Nyori, had done the same thing—sucked milk and life from her mother's breasts. She didn't believe it then. But what sweetness, what comfort she had found pillowing her head against mother's breasts, being rocked to sleep before a dying fire.

Studying the bear, she noticed that the beast's smooth hide was unbroken. She reached out with her burin and scratched a pointed mark to stab the flank, then stabbed into the shoulder, into the gut, into the hind leg. She pierced the upper back so powerfully that the lance shape came out the other side.

But this bear had no eyes. She saw that now. It would not even see what was happening. She scratched in the eye-circle, noticing then that the animal had no nostril with which to smell his own blood. She cut that in too, a half-circle like a real bear's nostril seen from the side. On the chest she scratched another circle—not an eye or nostril this time. No, this was a wound, the open wound of Scratcher's first lance thrust. She made another, then another, surprised to hear in her own throat a kind of growling like the bear's.

She scratched more stab marks. She scratched more circles, killing the bear, killing it, killing it. She scratched a circle over the heart, stabbing her point inside to kill the bear, to kill it at last, as the bear and Irta killed her mother. Blood had spurted from her mother's leg, so she made blood pour from the dead bear's mouth.

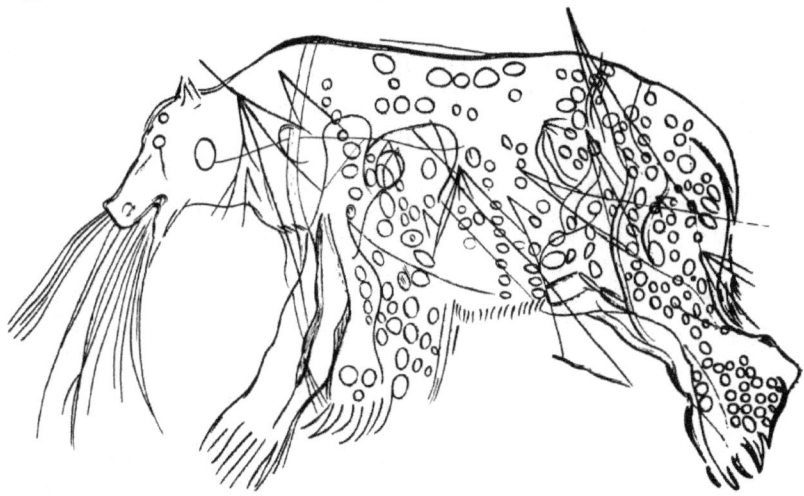

She was panting now, tears streaming on her cheeks, snot from her nose trailing onto her dirty chin. She wiped her eyes with the back of one hand, trying to look at the picture.

Once in butchering a reindeer, Nyori's flint blade had slipped and pierced a greenish bladder amid the guts. Green gall spilled out across the liver, spoiling the meat, tainting her hands. Later she rubbed her eyes with dirty fingers and felt the sting of the stuff. It was just the same now, tears burning like gall as they flooded from her eyes, a black bitterness draining out with them.

She looked at the picture and thought: Poor bear. Poor bear. He tried to get away. It wasn't the bear's fault. It wasn't Irta's fault either. It was Scratcher's fault—he said so himself. It was all his fault, and Nyori loved Scratcher. Suddenly, from behind her, from above her—echoing wildly in the chamber—came the chant of mourning.

"Ay-yi-yi-yi-yi! Ow-wo-wo-wo-wo!"

Not from her own throat. She spun around to see a pale face hovering in shadows ten steps away.

"Anzeel, you followed me again!" she shouted. "What do you

want? What? All right, I will! If you quit following me, I'll teach you how to scratch!"

"That's not why I followed you."

She saw then that his face shone in the lamplight, as wet from tears as her own. He knew what her bear picture meant. She lay one hand over her mouth, pressing her lips down so this time she wouldn't yell, then speaking quietly from behind it.

"I'll teach you, Anzeel. I will."

13

Then we fight!

As dawn slowly brightened the cave mouth, Drogben stood up against the light. Nyori saw his figure as a black shape, suddenly alert. He stared fixedly at something outside. Sliding backwards into the cave's smoky dimness, he stepped to the other side of the opening and again looked out.

Nyori sat up on her bison robe. Otti snored beside her with his mouth open, about to suck in a fluff of fur. She brushed it away and let her eyes fly back to the entrance. Drogben was gone. Already he had scuttled back into the cave, heading toward the nook where Kansi slept. Carrying her sandals by the laces, Nyori ran barefoot across cold cave dirt and got there first. She crouched beside her foster mother's grass pallet. When Drogben touched her arm, Kansi sat up instantly, staring into his sober face.

"What's wrong?"

"Something outside," he whispered. "I need your eyes."

Together they awakened Scratcher, and they all moved quickly back toward the entrance. Scratcher used his oak staff with its carved image of Irta, half as a crutch to steady his walk, half as a probe to pick his way through the shadowed cave. Kansi went ahead, moving far enough into the opening to see out. Nyori dropped her sandals and stayed just behind her, surprised that they permitted it.

"Yonder to the right," Drogben whispered, "see two boulders on the little ridge. Look between."

Then even Nyori could see it—an animal crouching flat to the ground, pointed ears upraised, fur spread in a brown pool against green grass. Nyori studied Kansi's eyes as they focused, eyes as clear as her son's—black centered, circled in blue rayed with gold. They were the best eyes in the Horse Band, sharp vision being one part of it, the other a mind that could tease meaning from the puzzle of things seen.

"It's a Wolf-Kill man," Kansi said. "He lay down there to spy on us last night and fell asleep. When the sun shines on him, he'll wake up and hide himself."

Nyori couldn't see all that in a patch of fur amid the grass. Neither could the others. They settled down to wait for the sun, which today would shine directly in through the cave mouth. This had been the prediction of Scratcher, who for years had charted on a bone movements of all the lights in the sky. Twice a year, once before its summer stand-still and once after, the sun reached in to the far wall of the first cave chamber. This was the second of the two days. Nyori sat with her back against rock, watching the sky beyond the entrance turn pale blue, then slowly deeper and darker as the sun crawled over the horizon. Smoke from a guttering fire in the cave thickened the air around her. A hand came down gently on her shoulder.

It was Anzeel, who had crept up quietly. She told him what his mother had seen. He placed his back against the rock and slid down to sit beside her. One boy hand rested on scuffed leather at the bent knee of his trousers. She picked it up in her own hand, clucking over the purple thumbnail.

"You hit yourself," she whispered. "You're stupid when you work flint."

She smiled sidelong at him and met his white smile, his glowing eyes. She didn't free the hand, liking it too much, even his calloused thumb with its bruised nail. Outside the cave lay danger, yet she felt strangely light, the same lightness that had filled her after she made the Deep Earth bear and then killed it.

For half a moon, she had been working in Deep Earth with Anzeel, teaching him how to scratch. He learned quickly, though, as she had told him, "You're not as good as I am." Again she turned to see his eyes. She couldn't stop smiling. Her eye did wander far enough to notice that Drogben was smiling too—smiling at them.

"Stop it!" Nyori hissed.

Drogben's eyes jerked away, and he wrestled his mouth back to a level line. Everybody had been making fun of Anzeel and Nyori. Drogben was just the worst. Nyori noticed now that Otti was just sitting up on the bison robe, sleepily scratching his blond head.

"Sssssst!"

Kansi's hand waved them all alert. Nyori glanced out to see the patch of fur suddenly hump up, a startled human face staring forward under the wolf headdress. The creature scuttled backwards, then sideways, to hide behind a boulder.

"What?" Scratcher said, blinking in confusion.

"It's a Wolf-Kill spy," Drogben told him.

"One only?"

"I'll go look."

"No," Scratcher said, "can't let them know we saw their spy."

"I go," Nyori said.

"Stop!" Scratcher rumbled. "We don't send a child."

"There's a hide in the tanning vat," she told him. "I'll go bring it in, that's all."

She was up and outside before anyone could object, blinking in the glare. She stumbled forward a few steps, then paused to let her eyes adjust as a little hand groped suddenly into her own.

"Otti!" she said.

He stood behind her, dancing from foot to foot.

"Need'a wet, Nyori. I need'a wet."

Far back in the cave's shadowed entrance, Kansi also did a little dance, a dance of frustration, tearing at her hair, pounding her head with the palms of both hands. Somehow the child had dodged past all the adults to run out. Nyori knelt and pulled Otti close.

"You can wet, but not in the regular place. Listen to me, Otti. We might see people hiding in bushes. Look at me, look at the ground, look at the sky. Don't look at them. Hear me? Don't look at them." Eyes widening, he blinked at her.

"Hear me?" Nyori asked again.

Breathlessly, he panted out his answer.

"Uh huh, uh huh, don't look."

She rose and took his hand, then walked briskly forward, feeling on her bare feet the warmth of yesterday's sun, still crawling up from the soil. Her eyes glanced lightly across the boulder, catching flashes of a sandaled foot, then a hand. The Wolf-Kill spy moved as she and Otti moved, trying to stay hidden from her. Otti was good, keeping his eyes on the ground. Quickly they reached the tanning vat, set in a level place just where the hill began its steep slope. She pointed.

"Do it there, Otti."

She bent to the vat and caught a red deer hide, raised and folded it double, oak water showering back into the hole. She held it nose high and folded again, her eyes searching out across the top of it. There! Below her in bushes on the slope, she saw movement, men sliding to the left and right. Her emergence had caught them by surprise. They were hiding themselves—many warriors. The hillside bristled with half-hidden lances and war clubs and axes. Some of these were the men who had chased the Cave-Brow down, killed him and then dragged his body away across the snow.

Then, as one figure scurried from bush to boulder, she saw a familiar face, a face scarred by its own mother. *Him.* And beside him an old man decked out in wolf cap and an eagle-winged tunic, like a wolf that could fly. Nyori tried to breathe smoothly. She hoped the pounding of her heart did not flutter the breast of her own tunic. Above the Wolf-Kills and beyond them, far beyond, the red sun boiled in a blue mist at the horizon. How many more suns would she see? With his back turned to his sister, Otti stared at another part of the sky as he finished peeing.

"Ahhhhhh," he sighed out his relief. "Ahhhhhh."

All the better, Nyori thought, because Wolf-Kills would be fooled by such an ordinary act.

"We go back now, Otti."

With the hide draped, cold and wet, across one arm, she swung around, feeling on the nape of her neck those many eyes. She took her brother's hand and walked slowly, stepping on her own shadow. Their two shadows stretched out long before them now as the sun's rays angled toward the cave mouth. When their shapes darkened the entrance, Scratcher reached hands out to find her. She placed herself within them.

"How many?" he asked.

"Many, many," she said, "must be all their men. No women, not that I could see."

The air went out of Scratcher with a whoosh.

"*All* the men! They will attack, and soon."

"Torfinn's with them."

The creaky bones of his hands tightened on her shoulders.

"Torfinn?"

"He led them here," Drogben said.

"He even picked his day," Scratcher said, ruefully shaking his head. "When they come into the cave, they have sun at their backs, we in our eyes."

"Someone was with him," Nyori told him, "an old man with eagle wings."

Scratcher looked at the earth, thoughtfully stroking his chin between thumb and forefinger.

"Yes. Skuuhl the Shuffler. So Torfinn went back to his father."

Quickly, Drogben ran to awaken Rothgar, who then rushed from pallet to pallet awakening the rest. People sat up, began tying on sandals, preparing themselves. Nyori sat at the smoky cave mouth to lace on her own sandals. The grown-ups were agitated, milling about as they talked, nervous feet raising little puffs of dust. Not Anzeel. He still sat calmly with his back against the wall, tracing a circle in the dirt with a piece of bone. Kansi was biting her lower lip, scraping it with the white line of upper teeth.

"We can't run," she said. "We'll never get around them out there."

"Then we fight!" Drogben growled.

"Yes," Scratcher said, "that way we kill a few of them, they kill all of us."

Drogben flung his hands out.

"What would *you* do, old man? Lie down and die!"

Just then Anzeel raised one hand dramatically high and jabbed the bone down at one edge of his circle.

"Here we are now, at Owl Cave entrance," he said. He dragged the point around the circumference. "This is the Hill. On the other side the river comes out." The point jabbed down again. "We go through Deep Earth and come out with the river on the other side."

Kansi shook her head, the violence of the gesture wracking her whole body.

"Not Deep Earth! Men go to Irta's womb. Never women!"

Anzeel jumped up and put his arm around her waist.

"Mother, you must. All the women."

"Not Deep Earth! No!"

Scratcher clasped his two hands, rubbing them together, then jerked them apart, staring into them as if somehow within their wrinkled palms lay the Horse Band's salvation. Drogben thudded the butt of his lance defiantly into dirt.

"We got our men, got three women who can fight. They won't forget we were here!"

Nyori moved close to Kansi and with one arm hugged her from the other side, boy and girl squeezing the woman between them.

"I go to Deep Earth," Nyori told her. "I'm a woman."

Nyori felt a shudder run through Kansi's body.

"Irta made you her child. Irta-child goes to the womb. Not other women. No!"

As Nyori studied Kansi's face, wondering how to convince her, the tanned skin of the woman's cheeks suddenly brightened. A blade of sunlight fell sidelong into the cave, casting flint-sharp shadows, showing up every scratch and scrape in rock of the one illuminated wall. Anzeel let go of his mother and raised a hand to shade his eyes, peering into the world outside.

"They coming?" Drogben asked.

"Not yet."

Scratcher didn't seem to see them now, didn't seem to hear. The old man stood centered in the cave mouth, his eyes wide and staring.

He threw up his arms, holding high the staff crowned with Irta. Oh, no! Nyori thought. He's doing his Mysteries again! His feet began bouncing in a slow dance, the Hopper dance. Beyond him, behind him, the sun had crawled onward so it now blazed almost full into the cave mouth. His head with its scraggly hair was crowned like the staff, but crowned with fire.

Around him the air burned, swirling with golden dust motes, with shining drifts of smoke—blinding bright, but also dark with the shadow Scratcher cast. It printed his skinny spread-eagled shape on the chamber's far wall above the Deep Earth Arch. Here was Scratcher at the entrance, yet there he danced on the cave wall. Between the two, quivering in the radiant air, stretched some invisible black part of him.

Nyori plunged her hand into that blackness and saw the hand disappear—almost disappear—withdrew and saw it take bright shape again, clenching and unclenching before her eyes. She knew better, of course she did, yet it seemed she had touched the old man's ghost.

"Women to my spirit!" the voice boomed out.

It was Scratcher's voice all right, but different. She'd heard this voice before. Throughout the great chamber, awe-stricken, open-mouthed faces turned to him.

"Only women! Women and girls! Stand within my spirit."

Men fell face down on the floor. Women walked as if asleep—women alone, women holding hands with daughters, two of them carrying babies. Most stepped into Scratcher's shadow and vanished. Yet when Kansi entered this black spirit, Nyori saw the woman's trembling silhouette against the cave wall on the other side. Nyori herself didn't move. The old man's body began a violent shaking, his shadow jerking in the air, jigging on the far wall.

"Eg-eg-eg-eg-eg-eg-eg...." Foam rose to his lips, dripped from his chin.

Now as he hopped Irta jolted him with her earthquake, the earthquake that terrifies all dwellers in caves—not that other members of the Horse Band could feel it. Now Irta sang out in a womanly voice through his mouth.

"I bless you, People of the Horse, giving you the Wolf-Kill coming as a sign. Always I welcomed your men to my heart, even to my very womb. This day you will *all* be born of it. Nyori was first.

99

Now to the others, other Women of the Horse, I command you: Come! Come now and be my children! All come to the safety of my womb!"

Unlike the other men, Anzeel had not prostrated himself. He glanced at Nyori. They stood looking somberly into one another. Then Anzeel's eyes swung away, toward some sound from outside the cave.

"They're coming," he said. "They're coming up the hill."

14

Battle Through Deep Earth

Scratcher's body lost its tenseness, began to sag as he turned back into himself, a hobbling and nearly blind old man. He led Kansi to Nyori.

"Take her. Get the other women. Through the Arch to Deep Earth."

Kansi seemed limp, her cheeks wetly shining.

"Oh, Nyori, isn't Irta good? Irta is *so* good..."

Still, Kansi was slow to give up the god's old laws. While the men prepared to fight, arming themselves, shouting encouragement to one another, the women grabbed up hides and spare garments and other belongings. It was their tanned leather, along with their lives, that the Wolf-Kills had come to steal.

Women raised firebrands above their heads, preparing for the darkness ahead. Amid the other children, Otti came carrying his and

Nyori's bed robe. Heavily laden, they all gathered outside the Arch but well back from it, standing in the blaze of sun that shone in. They eyed the blackness of Deep Earth as if it were the fanged maw of a cave lion.

War cries rang at the cave mouth. Nyori glanced over the women's heads and saw a little band of Wolf-Kills rush in. They cast a shower of lances and were met with few in return, badly aimed, thrown blindly against the light. Jeering, the Wolf-Kills darted out again into the mass of warriors marshaling just outside. Next time they would come in thick ranks, throw lances and close to kill with battle axes. Arrayed against them was that scattering of Horse Band men and Scratcher, who had put on his awkward reindeer headdress.

To the danger outside, the women paid no attention. Wolf-Kills were nothing compared to the terrors of Deep Earth. Kansi stood bravely at the front of the group, but when Nyori took her foster-mother's calloused hands, she could feel the shrinking back.

"Nyori, *I can't.*"

Under the sun-dazzled blonde crown of her hair, Kansi's eyes shone with belief. Nyori knew some beliefs were good, even necessary. This one could kill them all.

"Foster-mother, what did Irta say? 'I command you: come!'"

"You don't believe in Irta."

Holding the two hands, Nyori plunged backwards, her feet scrabbling in the dust. Kansi stood solid as a rooted tree. Beyond her, Horse Band men darted back and forth across the entrance, grabbing up fallen Wolf-Kill lances.

"Kansi, Anzeel will die if he fights against the light. Come to Deep Earth."

"I *can't,*" the woman groaned.

"This time I won't drag you. Close your eyes." After she closed them, Nyori tried to speak with the voice she had heard on Scratcher's lips, the voice of the god. "I command you: Come! Come be my children! All come!"

Kansi's arms relaxed, her hard hands yielding, stretching out before her. She had overcome belief, or started believing something new. Then the woman who had reared the child was led by that child, Nyori walking slowly backward through the Arch. Others followed, a hobbling old woman, young women tugging children along. As they ducked under, they huddled together, heads down, eyes squeezed shut. Their torches flickered on walls and ceiling of Deep Earth's first chamber. Kansi's hands had turned to ice. They shook spasmodically.

"Foster-mother, this is Deep Earth. Open your eyes."

Rock crystal blue eyes flicked open. Like a little girl awakening, Kansi stared about her in wonder but said:

"It's like the entrance chamber. Just smaller."

"Yes."

Nyori also trembled, weak with gratitude that she had been given power to make others do what was necessary. So this is why Scratcher believes, why he had to believe. Once more she felt that ache in her chest, that yearning, that hunger to believe in Irta. Irta is *so* good. But it was not Nyori who shouted out in celebration.

"Praise Irta!" Kansi said. "We live!"

At least for awhile, Nyori thought. With women and children now beyond the Arch, their men abandoned the cave mouth and fell back before the massed rush of enemies. A storm of Wolf-Kill lances thudded into the cave floor, shattered against rocky walls. The Horse Band men crowded through the Arch, arms loaded with Wolf-Kill weapons as if with firewood. Scratcher limped in behind them.

"Take torches deeper," he said. "We need dark here."

By now the sun's rays had slid away from the Arch. The attacking Wolf-Kills saw only dimness around them and a black hole ahead, from which—suddenly, violently—lances leaped out at them, their own lances. One Wolf-Kill fell screaming, his thigh pierced by a barbed point that would not pull out. Others dragged him away. They gathered in a grumbling crowd, white teeth bared under wolf headdresses. Out of the mass stepped Skuuhl in his eagle-winged finery and beside him, Torfinn, who waved a tattooed arm toward the Arch.

"Cowards!" he croaked. "Defiling Deep Earth with their filthy women's blood, their Evil Girl. Oh, Shufflers, Irta commands us: kill them!"

Not that Torfinn led the attack, but the next rush was hard to stop, three Wolf-Kills flinging themselves almost through the Arch before they all fell back. They left one man still on the ground. When it was over, Anzeel swung around, blood running from a wound on his brow.

"We can't hold here for long. Start the women back through the cave!"

By now the women had lighted oil lamps, which served better than torches for walking through cave darkness. Their yellow glow shone in Otti's scared eyes.

"Otti," Nyori said, "you know the Womb Shrine. Lead the women there."

"Womb Shrine?"

"Bawling Bison. Where the Bawling Bison is."

"Bawling Bison! Uh huh. I can, I can!"

He rose barely to the waists of the women, but they followed him, quickly disappearing down the passage. Kansi and Nyori and Riba stayed to battle alongside the men. The Horse Band fighters kept all the torches, using them one by one as they retreated. They would wait for the sound of Wolf-Kills creeping forward in darkness, then toss a torch among them to light targets for lances. Learning from that, the Wolf-Kills began to carry in pine branches, set them afire and throw them among their intended victims. That's when the rush always came, lean bodies hurtling from darkness, stabbing with lances, trying to close for the death struggle with axes.

The Horse Band fought off attack after attack. Grudgingly, Nyori began to admire Riba, who had tried to take Anzeel. With that hussy wielding a lance beside her, Nyori forgot jealousy. In one rush wilder than those before, a Wolf-Kill battered his way past Drogben and fell at her feet. Desparately, he crawled about, grabbing for the battle ax he had dropped. Nyori could have killed him with her lance. Without his wolf-mask, though, he was just another boy like Anzeel. She stomped the hand that groped for the ax. She kicked his shoulders, kicked his head, shrieking:

"Get out! Get out!"

He scrabbled sideways beyond her range, then leaped up and ran. Chamber by chamber, the Horse Band fell back through the cave, hard pressed, now fighting in light, now in utter darkness, sometimes in shadows more dangerous than the dark. Old Scratcher fought in the middle of his people, blindly hurling lances, his reindeer antlers bobbing crazily. The others shielded him. His presence steadied them and seemed to unnerve the Wolf-Kills, who shied away from his weakness to face tougher opponents.

The battle went well enough until Drogben took a lance thrust through his side. In the lull that followed, he turned to Nyori, swinging the butt of the lance in a slow arc, his right hand supporting the shaft so its leverage would not bear on his wound. His face pale and sweaty, he stood shakily before her.

"Pull out," he grunted.

The lance had cut through doubled leather tunics beneath the armpit, pierced his body and two layers of leather in back, where blood flowed now along the chipped flint edge and streamed to earth. Seeing his wound, Nyori felt the pain of it under her own arm. She called out:

"Scratcher, Anzeel, hold him."

Each grabbed an arm high up near the shoulder. Pulling, she felt sickening resistance as flint ground against bone. It didn't come free.

"Jerk!" Drogben said.

She leaned hard against the shaft and nearly fell as it yanked out. Blood gushed behind the point. Drogben grabbed the lance from her. He swung around to face the darkness from which the Wolf-Kills would come.

"Ready!" he said.

Abruptly, he sat down on the ground, held himself stiffly erect for a moment and then fell back, head thudding into dirt even as Kansi bent to catch it. He breathed in hoarse gasps. This had happened at the worst possible place, the Womb Shrine, where the cave widened enough to allow a mass attack by the Wolf-Kills. No one knew this better than Drogben.

"Leave me," he muttered. "Fight them here, and they kill us all."

Kansi knelt over him, cutting leather with a flint blade, peeling it back to see the wound.

"The blood, the blood…" she mourned. "But the point stayed outside the ribs."

Drogben's face was rigid, his eyes dry, while Kansi's tears rained down on it. She cut strips from his outer tunic to bind the wound, squeezing it tightly—the only thing she knew would hold in life's red juice. Rothgar moved agitatedly from foot to foot, as Otti did when he needed to pee.

"Drogben's right," he announced. "We can't carry him and stay ahead. They be on us."

It was truly the worst place, Irta's own womb, though it did surround them with pictures scratched by Steppe People Ancients. The scratchings were all there as Nyori remembered, animals climbing the walls, running, kicking, plunging. Once more she saw her own great bison bawling with its tongue thrust out, the old bull still recalling a stag deer he had seen long before—the memory that would last forever.

And near the chamber's ceiling, faintly visible amid shadows, she saw her own picture, the scariest one she'd ever made: Scratcher dancing in his reindeer costume, with upthrust hairy ears and tall branching horns. Out of the reindeer mask stared the eyes of Scratcher, wide, haunted eyes struggling to see through the white fog that was blinding him.

From the cold cave floor, Drogben grunted:

"Leave me. Get out!"

"Roll Drogben onto a hide and drag him," Nyori told them. "I'll stay with Scratcher and hold them."

"You and *Scratcher*?" Rothgar said.

The old man's watery eyes stared into Nyori. They could hardly see the shape of her face, yet he seemed to know her thoughts. He shrugged.

"Why not? We got no chance anyway without Drogben."

"*How* will you hold them?" Anzeel demanded. She looked into a boy's face bruised and scraped and blood smeared.

"The Mysteries," Nyori announced. "With the Mysteries." A crazy smile pushed itself out on her face. He grinned just as crazily back at her.

"I'll stay with you."

Soon the two Scratchers and Anzeel were left in the Womb Shrine. In the light of the torch she held, Nyori guided the old man to a little rise near the back.

"Stand here," she said. "Here you must dance for us. You're the Hopper. So, when I tell you, hop!"

He answered with booming solemnity.

"I OBEY, Scratcher Woman."

The reindeer antlers towered above his head, their forked shadows swaying as the torch flame dipped and flared. The lull lasted a moment longer. She heard the scrape of footsteps, the click of lance shafts against cave rock as they came. Anzeel stood to one side with his lance poised. Now neither Nyori nor the old man bore weapons. She felt her breath come quicker, her hand shake as it held the torch high.

The passage turned sharply just before it reached the Womb Shrine. Here the Wolf-Kills couldn't strike them by throwing from a distance. As Nyori expected, their first volley of lances clattered off one wall, glancing away to skid along the floor. Their warriors would have to gather where the passage opened out and then rush forward with axes.

A big pine branch soared, flaming, into the Womb Shrine, bounced down from a ceiling projection and crashed at Nyori's feet. Its light far outshone her torch, showing up the painted faces of Wolf-Kills as they massed at the entrance, blinking in sudden brightness. The throng of warriors parted. That old man wearing the eagle-winged tunic pushed his way through. He must be a fighter, Nyori thought, because one wing had been hacked away, the other de-feathered at the tip. It was Skuuhl, the Horse Band's old enemy. His eyes seemed keen enough as they roved the chamber, searching for victims of their next assault.

"Scratcher, dance!" Nyori cried. "Hop, hop, hop!"

He danced, lifting one foot high and then the other, bending and bobbing, mostly hopping but sometimes shuffling a little, his shadow dancing with him against the stone surround. The Wolf-Kills jeered. Their laughter roared through the Womb Shrine, echoed and echoed once again. But their leader didn't laugh.

"Hopper blasphemy!" Skuuhl raged. "Defilers of Deep Earth! Kill them!"

Nyori tossed away her own puny torch and grabbed the pine branch. Turning it so a big cluster of needles would catch afresh, she raised it into high spaces of the cave. Breathing the scent of hot pine resin, she saw firelight blaze suddenly on old Scratcher, the weak and fleshly Scratcher, and also on that other Scratcher, the one above who would dance forever.

Those glittery Wolf-Kill eyes also saw the eternal Scratcher, who turned his face full toward them, transfixing them with round owl eyes. Their grins died on their faces. Their teeth were bared no longer in ferocity but, suddenly, in terror. Skuuhl lay the back of one bloody hand against his forehead and stared beneath it at the horror.

"Ga!" he choked out. "Gug-ga-ga!"

He was first to break. He swung around and smashed through the line of them, knocking one man down and trampling across him.

"Eeeee-e-e-e-e-e!" another yelled. They fought each other for room to turn, jammed themselves tight into the passage opening. One warrior dragged another back and squeezed through. Then the clot freed itself and they were gone, screaming as they fled back through the cave.

The Horse Band did not pause to celebrate. Along the passage leading from the Womb Shrine, Rothgar had already picked up one corner of the hide on which Drogben lay. Three others took hold. They lifted him and moved swiftly deeper into the cave.

Those bearing the litter threaded the wounded man up one of the cave's marrowbone passages, carefully down the next. After that, the way was smoother. The patter of many footsteps rang hollow at places on the rock, where holes led downward to lower galleries. Through the holes Nyori heard the river's whisper below, breathed its moist breath—fresh amid the staleness of ancient air.

Once again, Nyori saw the first big picture she had ever scratched, of the little mare colt she and Anzeel had killed, saw how she sketched the mare's small muzzle and deep jaw, the tenseness of all her legs. Anzeel eyed it as they passed. Where the tunnel widened, he stopped at a bare place on the rock and pulled Nyori aside to let others go by.

"Hold the lamp for me," he said, a grin spreading on his face above the flame of the lamp he held. He had washed the blood away with water from a cave pool, but the raw gash still marked his brow. He took a flint burin from his pouch and stepped up to the rock. He scratched with great freedom, hardly looking at the stone, feeling rather than seeing the sweep of his stroke, wrist smoothly throwing curves. Finishing, he stepped away. Nyori moved close, perhaps too close to see.

"What is it?"

Anzeel kept grinning at her.

"If you have to ask, I need to get better at this. Come on," he said, taking her hand.

Soon they caught up. They passed through the chamber with folded ceiling, like the ice-white folds of a winter tent, saw again the many teeth-that-grow, white fangs in the wet mouth of an animal. As they neared the outlet, the river's whisper became a roar. Their lamps shone on foaming water. Then Nyori heard the voice that had been silenced.

"Put me down."

"You can't walk," Kansi said.

"Down!" Drogben growled.

They put him down. He rolled over on the hide, using his hands to push himself slowly upright. With the bleeding stopped, Drogben had come back to himself. He stood there teetering before them.

"I just wanted an easy ride," he said, a little smile growing on his lips.

At that, they jeered him. Then Kansi led him down to the river. She stayed with him through the passage out of the cave. Since it was fall and the river low, they could breathe all the way, at times floating, at times bouncing along the rocky bottom with the current. Weak as he still was, Drogben tried to become once more a battle leader. When daylight began to shine through the water around their feet, he called to the fighters ahead:

"If Wolf-Kills are there, we must see them first."

Emerging, they saw not Wolf-Kills but instead the sun of afternoon burning through a yellow veil of clouds. They saw trees along the river course, daylight blazing on water there as it tumbled over rocks. They saw thorn rose again, not blooming now but with leaves golden in the light. They saw green hills rolling to the far horizon. None of it had to be lit by lamps. They sucked in air, not flower scented but sweet with the smell of grass. Her face wet with tears, Kansi stood on the riverbank and spoke to the women around her.

"We came through Deep Earth, through Irta's womb. We are born again. Now we too are her children. Irta is good! She is *so* good!"

The other women and half the men wept with her, rubbing their eyes, blowing their noses. Drogben's tears came faster than his woman's, but he took her hand.

"Move!"

He was still weak, but he walked with Sudrog steadying him on one side, Kansi on the other. Laden with dripping bundles of leather, they walked mostly without talking. Occasionally Anzeel stopped to glance back. They had crossed three little hills when, as the sun slid beneath the horizon, he again turned.

"Look!"

Far, far behind, the first Wolf-Kills had reached the place where the river came out of the hill. These half-dozen had run ahead of their band. At this distance they seemed mere ants, scurrying around the rocky opening in the hillside. So they had found it, the Horse Band's path to safety. Now they knew that Owl cave was open all the way through the hill. But the knowledge came too late, Nyori thought. Drogben looked back at their angry searching and, for all his weakness, roared:

"Ha! Ha!"

Because they were free. Leading the march, Old Scratcher angled more toward the Cold Sky. It was time anyway to move down from the mountains toward winter quarters at the Shelter. Nyori saw the old man speak to Rothgar, who then stepped out of line so the rest could pass. As Rothgar dropped behind her, she felt his oaken hands grip her waist, felt herself soar into the air, rising over his head to come down—bump!—on the man's thick shoulders.

"Scratcher Woman!" he bawled out.

Anzeel's rough hand with its bruised thumbnail snaked out to grab her bare ankle.

"Scratcher Woman!" Anzeel yelled, as others took it up.

Anzeel had called her that—and for the first time. Anzeel! From his rough grip on her ankle, Rothgar's warmth seemed to rush upward through her body. She squeezed Rothgar's head between two hands to hold herself and thought again of god Irta, riding her hairy mammoth. Was it god Irta in whom she now believed? No, it was herself.

Anzeel's hand tightened on her ankle, released and gripped again. He turned a closed-mouth, jaunty smile up to her, the pleasure of the moment squeezing his eyes nearly shut. At that moment Nyori

recognized what Anzeel had that day scratched on the cave wall, something he had seen reflected in river water, or by lamplight in the clear pools of Deep Earth. Now she remembered his picture: a face! A face roughly drawn but still deft. Like herself, Anzeel was no longer afraid to scratch people. His picture was more real than any human thing Nyori had ever made.

111

"You scratched your own face!" she yelled at him. "It was good, Anzeel! But, watch me, I can scratch people better than that!" He let go of her ankle and leaped sideways, staggering as if she'd struck him.

"Ah! Ah! Scratcher Woman is jealous!" He groaned, and he grinned. "The great Scratcher Woman is jealous."

She turned her face forward so she wouldn't have to see him, feeling the sudden coolness of air on that ankle. Her body still boiled with heat. Now it was the heat of irritation.

She would show him. She would teach him, and still she would be better.

15

Now, Her Own Blood

They slept a few uneasy hours that night, then woke before dawn to hurry on through the next day. Ahead, the hills kept rising only to fall away, each new hill lower than the one before. Day by day the season cooled; day by day they walked toward the Cold Sky. Yet as they descended, the air grew warmer. The Blue Mountains were always colder than lower country. The Horse Band knew this, as did bison and horse and cattle. Ahead of the people, great herds migrated, leaving piles of dung to steam in the morning air.

The Horse Band had meat to eat, also fruits of waning summer—sour hawthorne, grapes ripened to bruised purple, sour and sweet in them mingling as Nyori popped one and then the other between her teeth and spat the seeds. Once they stopped in a field of coarse grasses. She scrubbed seed heads between her palms. Puffing her cheeks, she blew husks away and took a mouthful of seeds, chewing slowly, feeling the stickiness develop, the grainy taste turning slowly sweet on her tongue. Others around her did the same. They spent a whole day in that field, eating and filling pouches with harvested grain.

This was friendly country, full of the Steppe People. They met other bands, trading hides, trading firestones mined in the mountains for lowland products and mammoth ivory that mostly came from the grassland steppe that lay toward Sunrise Sky.

Nyori rose early one morning to gather firewood before the others wakened. She felt a dark heaviness in her gut, as if she'd swallowed her own firestone, its brazen taste raw in her throat. Had she eaten bad meat? She had no energy to pull on her leather trousers. She wore only her long leather tunic. With rolling prairie all around, white dawn just brightening its far edge, she picked her way up a brushy draw. She was heaping her right arm with fallen branches when she saw a meandering line of blood on her right leg.

With two fingers she drew the leather flap of her tunic aside. A fat droplet trembled at the end of the line, a black-red bead on the scuffed knob of her ankle. Had she stabbed herself with a thorn? She lifted the flap and saw the droplet's shining trail leading upward on the pale inside of her thigh. She felt a trembling in her jaw, that brazen burning now deep in her gut. She was *bleeding,* her own blood now. For the first time, she was bleeding that way. Nyori set down her armload of branches.

She knew all about this, of course, how soft grass blades could be bunched and braided into a swatch of thick rope, doubled and redoubled, making a pad to absorb the blood. Often she'd made such ropes for older women. It was easy enough to braid one for herself and place it. Finished, she sat down on a boulder. The sun had risen half above the horizon, high enough so she could feel its faint warmth on her bare legs, now quite free of blood. Down the draw below her, another early riser had stoked last night's fire. A tang of smoke rose to where she sat.

She was bleeding. Now more than ever she must not touch Anzeel. If he asks again, she dare not become his woman. To be burdened, to be borne down, to be stopped from her scratching in Deep Earth, and with every moon to bleed again. Again and again. In advanced age some women got past it, but few lived so long. That darkness still dragged at her gut.

"Women with their blood!" Torfinn had screamed at her. Women with their dirty blood. Then, as Drogben had pointed out, Nyori had been too young for blood. No more. Now she had it, and she could have children. She wanted to make pictures in Deep Earth. She didn't want children. She didn't *want* to bleed.

She sat there till the sun broke free of earth to show itself full face, blazing white, yet not so white you couldn't stare into it. Arms crossed before her breasts to hug herself, she rocked to and fro on the boulder, watching the it climb up the sky, until from far below she heard the calling.

"Nyori! We need the wood. We need to cook and start on the trail."

After half a moon of slow travel, the Horse Band came to a place where two rivers flowed down from a range of hills and became one. Old Scratcher spoke to Drogben, then stepped off the path and waited for Nyori and Anzeel, whom he pulled aside. His hand showed the young people how the joined waters rolled out across almost flat country toward the Sunset Sky. He swung around and gestured up the left river fork, which rose through a green valley into hills.

"We three go upstream," he told them.

"Only us?" Anzeel said.

"Drogben leads others to the Shelter. We'll go there too. First I want to show you something."

They labored far up the river fork to reach that something, arriving almost at dark to set their baggage down beside a wide downward funnel in the earth. Despite his dimming vision, Scratcher then managed to strike a spark to make a fire. He fed twigs to the blaze until larger branches caught. With a flint knife, he began cutting torches.

"I lead!" Anzeel yelled. "I go down first.".

He grabbed up the first torch and slid down the funnel into a small hole that led off one side. He was gone before Nyori could object. Hardly had Scratcher lighted the second torch when Anzeel soared out of the hole. His feet scrabbled for a grip on the earth.

"Bear! Bear!"

The feet took hold, scattering rocks that tumbled away behind him. He raced to the baggage and grabbed up his lance, swinging around to stand between the others and whatever might come out. Scratcher spoke to his back.

"How you know it was bear?"

"I smelled him. I saw his eyes."

115

Anzeel panted so hard he could barely get the words out. Watching, Nyori felt an ache around her heart—that he could be so scared yet make a stand, the lance head trembling as he held it before him. They waited a long time, until Nyori got sick of watching a silly hole.

"You really saw bear?"

"Yes!"

Then the darkness of the hole welled upward as a black shape grew out. It kept growing, this huge huge blackness squeezing up from what had seemed a tiny opening. The bear clambered lightly to the far lip of the funnel and swung around to face them. Anzeel cocked the lance back on a thrower. Nyori grabbed up her own lance and moved beside

him. A cool hand closed on her arm. Scratcher had reached out to both of them.

"Don't."

So they didn't throw. The bear watched them, eyes shining, fur glossy in evening light as he rocked nervously back and forth on flat feet. His panting seemed to heat the evening air. His odor, musty from the cave, blew to them on a little breeze. His big eyes stared at them, his mouth half-open as if laughing at their fear. Was he like the bear that mauled Scratcher, that killed Nyori's mother? This one seemed almost to be saying hello, pretending to be friendly because he was more scared than the people. Instantly, in her mind Nyori saw the bear she would scratch.

For a long moment, they faced the animal. Then Old Scratcher threw up one arm.

"Leave us!"

The bear did. He swung around and padded away, the fleshy soles of his feet flapping up as he lifted them delicately and put them down. To Nyori, this seemed a triumph for Scratcher—the bear obeying his command—but the old man stood there trembling worse than Anzeel had, sighing out long breaths.

"This," he said, "this is what I should have done for the bear that killed your mother."

When the old man recovered, he led them down the funnel, his torch sending smoke up into Nyori's face. Scratcher gave her his torch, hung by one hand from a ledge and dropped into blackness below, landing with a thump.

"Drop your lights, then come!" he yelled, and echoes rang up.

They did as he ordered, dropping into the cave and quickly grabbing up their guttering torches. Cave air cooled her tongue as her mouth fell open. This was not like Owl Cave, all twisting passages and cramped, small spaces. This chamber reached high and stretched far. Its rough walls slanted outward at first, then curved inward to meet the arch of rock overhead. In the middle the ceiling bubbled downward in a boiling storm cloud of stone. Between the rough walls and that storm cloud ceiling, wide expanses of bare rock shone in torchlight like the inside of a clam shell.

"Perfect!" Nyori shouted, "*perfect* for pictures!"

"Look!" Scratcher said.

Two young heads dropped back. Above them on the left, a huge bull had been painted—*painted*—far bigger than a real bull. Its black outline raged across the gleaming surface, head thrown up with twice-curved horns lifted high, the line of its back sweeping far to the right. The bull seemed so alert and alive.

"He's strong," Anzeel murmured.

"Legs too short, too stiff," Scratcher said. "That's what I thought when I finished it. Now all I see is a blur."

"Beautiful," Nyori breathed.

117

A smile lighted the old man's face. He trembled with pleasure at their words, the great Scratcher trembled, his hands moving jerkily. That he cared what they said made her proud, yet sad that their judgment now meant so much to him.

"I painted it when I knew my eyes were leaving. Last chance."

"Did you do it to for Irta?" Anzeel asked.

Scratcher looked at his feet.

"Not for Irta. I was alone. Nobody here to dance for Irta. No Mysteries."

"Why?" Nyori demanded. With the toe of one sandal, he stirred the dust of the floor. He shrugged and kept looking at the floor. "You made it because you wanted to!" Nyori accused. "For *fun*, that's why."

He looked shame faced but answered defiantly.

"Not your concern!"

Suddenly panting, eager as the good-natured bear, Nyori sucked in his words.

"Oh, Scratcher, me too!   That's why I do it."

Piously, the old man raised one finger before her face.

"But also for Irta. We got to remember Magic and Mysteries."

She was hardly listening. Except for this bull, the cave was empty. Nyori stared about her at the huge expanse of wall and ceiling. *Empty!*

"What's its name, this cave?"

"No name.   None I know."

"Then it's Empty Cave," she said, "because you left it almost empty. Who paints the rest?"

He started climbing an incline of loose dirt toward the opening to outside. Perhaps he had not heard her question.

"Who?" she roared at him. WHOOO...OOOO... rang the echo. A cave owl's question. He stopped and looked at them, frowning to hide the smile that struggled in the corners of his mouth.

"First we go to the Shelter. You learn more, better to use paint. Next fall we come back, spend winter here. And this..." He waved both hands at the crystalline expanse above. "...belongs to Nyori and Anzeel."

16

Ugly, and Awful, and Wonderful

The walls of the Shelter were of gnarled and crumbly rock, bad for pictures. She found a ledge of stone up the valley, also gnarled but not crumbly. She and Anzeel made many trips, carrying home flat rocks cradled between them in a hide, leaning outward against the weight.

Day following day, the fall sun reached farther into the Shelter, warming them as they worked. This was no cave—just a deep rock overhang high enough to stand in. With its back to cold winds, it opened toward Warm Sky on a creek that had worn its own gentle valley, laced with bare branches of alder, ash, and oak, where dried red currants still nodded on the vines and the soil was thick with garlic to season their meals of meat.

First she scratched the bear, the grinning bear that had so frightened them at Empty Cave. She used the bear picture to teach Anzeel, showing him how he must take chances, throw lines out freely. He watched as she tried it several times, only on the last rock tablet beginning to get it right.

This was the bear that killed her mother, it was the bear she had scratched on the wall at Owl Cave and stabbed and killed. It was also a new bear, reshaped today with quick strokes of her burin. She tried to catch his amiable grin as he rocked on claw-toed feet, afraid and pretending not to be. Looking into the face of her reborn bear, Nyori felt in her chest a sweetness, a completeness. And she was finished with hatred of bears, though not her fear of them .

One morning she glanced up and saw Drogben standing just outside the Shelter. He stared keenly toward glittering wavelets of the creek, faintly smiling, as if he'd seen salmon running there—not that salmon come upstream in autumn. Anzeel had scratched his own face on the wall as they left Owl Cave. She had vowed to draw better faces. Drogben would be first—his face and head from the side. On a flat stone she cut in his nose, just for fun making it extra long. She swooped out his jaw to make what was strong in reality even stronger. Drogben's chin

bristled with short beard stubble. To make him more handsome, she left the whiskers out.

Except for Anzeel's rough sketch—hardly recognizable as human—she had never seen a picture like the one she was making. How would her people take it? This thought caused the hooked point of her burin to pause an instant above the stone. Then she cut again. After all, Torfinn was no longer here to oppose her. She put in Drogben's funny smile and drew the eye that had seen so many fights. She noticed that she was drawing not what she now saw—his eye from the side—but what she best remembered, the eye's wide lance-point shape as seen from the front. Like the eye on her bison spear thrower. Face from the side, eye from the front. A shadow fell across the sketch. Nyori looked up at Riba just as the woman pointed to the tablet and yelled:

"Ey-yaaaaa! Drogben!"

Others came running, Rothgar and Kansi little Otti. Others too. They gathered chattering behind her as Nyori cut the last lines, two descending scratches to sketch the throat, hints of wrinkles around nose and eyes.

Nyori heard Drogben's voice boom out behind her.

"Not me!"

"You!" Riba yelled, swinging around to the others. "Look at him, the fool. He's seen his face in water, but never from the side." Slowly the hairy man's real face changed, cheeks sagging, the great jaw dropping as his mouth widened. With a sharp intake of breath, he saw it, he recognized himself. His hands shot out to grab the stone. Nyori was jerked to her feet, dragged halfway from the shelter toward the sunlight that blazed outside. He was headed for the trash pit on the slope below.

"Stop, Drogben!"

"I smash!"

"Don't!" She caught him unawares, jerked back and forced him to stop. "All right, that *is* you. What will happen if you smash the stone?"

He panted in agitation, his slow-blinking eyes darkly clouded.

"Let go," she begged. "I'll take care."

Kansi came up beside him, laying hands on his thick arms. He looked pitifully into Kansi's eyes.

"Me! Me! What happens when it breaks?"

"Nothing!" Nyori groaned. "I asked you what will happen because I wanted you to stop. It's not you, it's your *picture*."

His pleading eyes swung back to Nyori.

"Remember Irta," he said, almost chanting the old words, "Remember, Deep Earth is her womb, everything gets born of it. Whatever we scratch on the walls, those things appear on the prairie above, on the tundra, in the forest when reindeer and bison and horses drop their young."

Belief burned in his eyes.

"Drogben, look!" Nyori swung her hand toward blinding sunlight just beyond the overhang. "This is not Deep Earth, and this—she shook the stone tablet they both now held—this is not a wall picture."

In the bafflement of his face, she could see one part of his mind slide against another. As his fingers loosened, she pulled the tablet free and leaned it against a boulder. She felt the hairy man's heavy presence as he knelt at her side and stared broodingly at his image. Kansi put out her hand to caress the stubble along his jaw.

"The picture makes you handsome," she told him.

When Drogben again reached toward it, Nyori yelled, "Don't!" Then she shrugged and gave him the tablet.

Gingerly, he rotated it slowly leftward to stare edgewise, straight into the nose.

"My other eye?   Where?"

"It's a picture from the side, Drogben. But I can draw you that way, with both eyes."

"No!" He turned the stone back, staring thoughtfully into his own full profile. Then he glanced up at Kansi. "Handsome?"

"Yes! Very handsome."

Drogben returned the stone to Nyori and with great dignity strode away. The others edged closer, still wary. As they bent to see, murmuring among themselves, Nyori studied those faces she knew better than her own, faces dear to her. One was Anzeel's. He came forward and knelt, staring into the picture of Drogben.

"My face," he said, "the one I scratched in Owl Cave, it was a mess," he said. "I'll never be able to do this."

"You're better now."

She wanted him to get better, of course she did—just not better than her. That thought darkened her mood. Would she always be this way? Jealous. Grudging. Would she never never stop? As if he knew her thoughts, he said:

"I throw the lance better."

She grinned.

"Teach me. I'll beat you!"

He inclined his head toward the picture.

"Nyori, it's fine."

Anzeel's face was dull as dirt, faint muddy fingerprints marking his cheeks. To her it seemed to shine, his clear, open gaze burning on her skin. Once more she felt twisted inside, twisted and tight and grudging—yet suddenly so broken by his words that her eyes filled, so shamefully pleased she couldn't look at him. Nyori rose and fled into the sunlight, running blinded down toward the creek, hearing behind her Anzeel's plaintive question.

"What did I do now?"

Remembering all those faces she knew better than her own, Nyori one by one began to cut them into stone. First Scratcher. She recalled the instant he had thrown up his hands and wiggled fingers, calling forth Mysteries to bring the lost children back from the depths of the cave. Now she scratched the picture which so long ago had flashed on her mind. That was one dear person.

Another was Otti. The three of them, Nyori and Anzeel and her brother, again went up the valley for tablets of stone. Climbing the ledge, Otti slipped off, bounced once against the rock face and fell into Anzeel's arms. Blood oozed from the skin of his hands, scraped thin by rock, scraped through in places. He cried for awhile but then struggled to calm himself. Anzeel dried the tears with his own fingertips and patted Otti's cheeks. Then the child looked gratefully up at Anzeel, even smiled.

That's how Nyori caught him in the picture, her brother's lips fighting to hold the smile, his fine hair trailing behind his head. This time she thought more about the eye. She scratched it—not as a wide spear point, the eye as seen from the front—but as she had actually seen it from the side, more like a hazelnut. She left out only the tears and dirt on his cheeks. Finished, she showed it to her brother.

"Who?" she asked him. He had heard his sister ask the same question of others and so knew the answer.

"Me?" His brown eyes traced the line around the profile of his nose. "I look good!" Nyori had shown him his own best side, had done a fine thing for him

"You are good," she said. "You are *so* good."

She grabbed him and hugged him to her, tasting salty boy as she kissed his forehead, kissed his ear, kissed his dirty cheek. She loved the child in him and, still squeezing him breathless, suddenly wondered whether some day

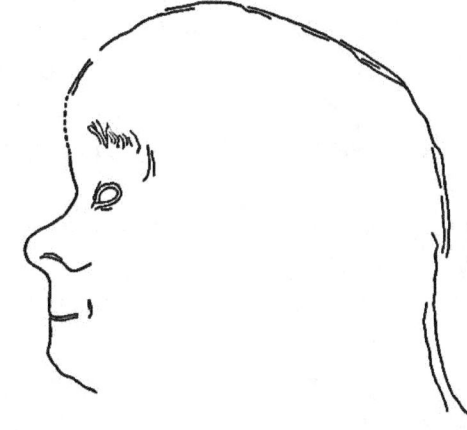

she herself might make a child, a real child.

Like others, Old Scratcher seemed stunned by the appearance of human faces on stone. Still, he kept teaching Nyori and Anzeel. He showed them how to grind ocher, changing its color with the heat of a fire to make yellow, red, deep orange. He took charcoals from the fire for black, taught them how to mix the powders with animal fat and make paints. Under his direction, they painted a few stone tablets. Mostly he worked to free the lines of their scratchings. With his wrinkled paw, he would grab the young hand that held the burin and shake it, shake off cowardice, then guide the hand in throwing out a line, later to be scratched deeper into the stone.

Nyori came quietly up behind Scratcher one day as he squatted before her picture of him. He was trying to decipher with fingertips faint lines he couldn't see with his eyes. Somehow he knew she was there.

"You caught me," he said. "In stone. Should I yell like Drogben?"

She smiled.

"You said it was dangerous for me to scratch anything. Does this scare you?"

"Yes! It's strange. I walked to White Mountains, far toward Sunrise Sky. I walked toward Cold Sky till I touched the Great Ice. I walked to the Warm Sea and waded. Salty water! I saw many caves, painted and scratched. A few times I saw people carved in mammoth ivory, mostly women. *Never* with faces—nor even hands or feet. No, yours are first, first like this. First true pictures of people."

"I don't think they're dangerous," Nyori said.

"Something might happen," he murmured.

"Something!" she sighed. "Something always happens."

Slowly the Shelter filled up with pictures. Nyori made one of Kansi, showing how she had knelt, praying to Irta before the Deep Earth Arch. Anzeel scratched Mayro and then Rothgar, both awkward sketches but still recognizable. It all went smoothly until the day they began setting up the pictures in a row along one wall. It was too much for Rothgar when his own pointy-bearded, pointy-nosed face appeared in that gallery.

He moved out of the Shelter, said he wouldn't sleep where people were being recreated before his eyes—where he himself had been created a second time. He carried his goods to a shallow overhang around the cliff corner. Three mornings later, after the first big storm of winter, he wakened under his bison robe, clawed his way up and found himself standing neck deep in drifted snow. He came back to sit before the Shelter fire, grumbling but resigned to living with these duplicate members of his band.

As winter deepened, the men cut slim, nearly limbless alder trunks from a thicket. In a corner of the Shelter, the band erected a lean-to frame, over which they stretched hide of bison and reindeer. Even with a fire inside, it was so cold Nyori's breath smoked before her face, yet still the warmest place in this frozen world. Now and then Anzeel or Nyori would drop a pine branch on the fire, tilting their stone tablets so the crackling needles would light their work

All winter they scratched like that while others took care of them, as if they possessed some magic—this Scratcher Woman and the young man Anzeel. When Anzeel did hunt, he went out with Drogben just for sport. The older man was still best where power was needed, as in thrusting through the bunched muscles of bison. On distant kills with his spear thrower, still weighted with her tiny bison sculpture, Anzeel proved himself better. Nyori went with them one day to learn the thrower.

They stood on an icy cliff side as Anzeel showed her how to grip the thrower's handle, hooking its point into the hollowed butt of the lance. Late in the day, with a little clatter on the rocks, an Ibex ram appeared atop a boulder. Trembling, wide-eyed, the ram watched them.

"Try it," Anzeel whispered.

She tried. The thrower lifted the lance shaft high above her head, her lengthened reach thrusting it violently forward. She could feel the extra power her bison-sculpture weight added to the throw. The lance flew far but still fell short. Flaring, the Ibex danced away over the ice, pausing at the cliff corner to take a last look at the humans. Drogben handed Anzeel his own lance.

"You!" Drogben barked.

"I can't reach him."

"Try."

Anzeel grunted as his throwing arm blurred in Nyori's vision. She couldn't even follow the lance flight—just suddenly, magically, the ram tumbled backwards, skidded, bounced down the cliff side trailing blood. Anzeel was the son of Drogben's woman, but he was not Drogben's son. Why, then, was the Hairy Man so proud as he and Anzeel marched together into the Shelter?

"I walked out his cast." The older man exulted. "Sixty long steps!" He squatted to grab Anzeel at the hips, lifted him so both the young man's head and the ram on his shoulders bumped the Shelter's ceiling. "The boy can throw!" Drogben boomed. "I can't throw so well."

This was the Horse Band's great hunter, the best, saying he was no longer best. His statement was surely good for the Horse Band if not for Drogben, Nyori thought. How could he do that? How could Drogben be so generous? She herself was not that way.

So much had happened to Nyori since they last made this trip, she felt exhausted by it. Still there were things to do here, things to learn. On the pitted face of a stone, she scratched her own face, deliberately making it look the way she felt— the mouth and eyes weary. It was not the face of Nyori now but instead how she might look at Kansi's age. Because that's how she felt. Amazing, she thought, how pictures let you travel ahead in time or drop back to long-past days. Anzeel laid aside the triangular chunk of stone he'd been working and leaned to look over her shoulder.

"She looks like you," he said, "just tired."

"I feel that way."

Beyond Anzeel, a gray mist of rain half hid the thicket on the far shore of the creek, which was out of its banks now, washing the meadow below the Shelter. Daylight flooded across him toward Nyori, but in the darkened face she saw his eyes brighten.

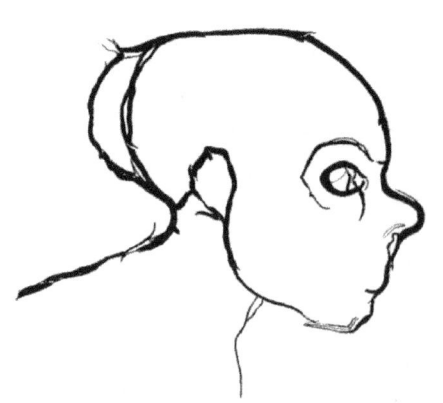

"Then let me be your man. You be my woman."

She felt the little

smile inside, but her lips did not widen.

"Will that rest me?"

He looked at the floor, stirring dirt there with his finger.

"We might have a child. Might be *harder*."

"Then how will it help, me being your woman?"

"I'll help you. I will."

"You already help me."

She leaned behind him and caught one corner of the triangular stone he'd been working.

"What are you scratching?" she demanded.

His hand jerked out and pressed the rock tight to earth. She couldn't budge it.

"I'm not finished."

"I want to see."

He wouldn't let go. Nyori's eyes glanced suddenly over his shoulder, toward the brightness at the Shelter's entrance. Just outside, Mayro sat chewing the corner of a hide to soften it. Everyone else was out foraging.

"Drogben caught a salmon!" Nyori shouted. "Are salmon running so early?"

Her trick never seemed to fail. Anzeel spun around to look, and the tablet came loose. She dragged it into her lap, tilting it so the light would fall sideways across the figures.

"Don't!" Anzeel had turned back, jumped to his feet and now stood indignantly over her. "I told you, it's not finished." She sat staring at Anzeel's faint lines scratched into the surface—quick, sweeping curves, the sort old Scratcher liked—feeling their simple power as a tightness around her heart. He had pictured

her with long hair, as she used to wear it, as he'd always liked it.

"It's finished enough for me," Nyori said.

He didn't argue any more. He just stood before her, not saying anything. Her eyes yearned above the two figures, tried to search out their meaning. Anzeel loved Irta, deeply believed in Irta. Nyori would never believe. Always there would be that difference between them. Still, she said:

"All right, Anzeel, you be my man. I'll be your woman."

By now the heaviest snows were past, days slowly lengthening as winter shaded off toward spring. Still it snowed, often only a few big flakes that hung long in the air, floating sideways far back into the Shelter as if seeking her out. Nyori caught a snowflake, which turned to water on her fingertip. She licked the water and in it tasted clear air. Through spaced snowflakes she could see the curving blackness of the creek, already free of ice, an alder thicket crowding the far bank.

Then came a single day of sun and several of clouds before the rain started. It wasn't a hard rain, just steady, this rain that told them spring was nearly here. People began to shift about, gather the things they had scattered through the Shelter. When the weather dried, they would start the march back to the Blue Mountains, the same journey they had made in past years, and their parents, and those who came before.

At last came a day so warm they worked outside the hide tent. She saw Anzeel's shoulders jerk forward, saw the muscles of his forearm ridge up as he slashed at the stone tablet braced between his knees.

"Move it easy," she instructed. "Don't clutch so. Remember what Scratcher said—free and easy."

He gouged again, going over and over the line, cutting deeper. Then his burin turned a corner. She saw it was the forehead and nose of a face, the latest cut angling back to the upper lip. The stone was so broken there wasn't even room for the crown of this person's head.

"Not so deep, Anzeel. You'll ruin it."

He didn't seem to hear. His own face was ridged like his arms, wrinkled in furious concentration. He reached across to where the right ear would be and cut another groove, the twice-curved line of the lower jaw. From the way he sawed at the stone, he might have been cutting the man's throat. In just such vicious strokes she had long ago scratched the bear that killed her mother.

"What are you doing? Don't!"

"Shut up! Leave me alone!"

She was his woman, but this offended her. He went on slashing the rock, shaping the domed line of the skull as it curved downward, then inward to become the neck. Torfinn! It was Torfinn, with a face stretched long to make him wolfish.

"You ruin the burin," she told him.

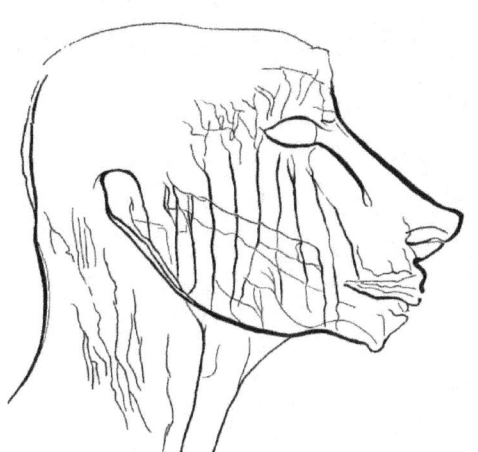

"Leave me alone."

He cut in the eye—the eye from the front in a face seen from the side.

"That's all wrong," she said. He paid no attention. The flint point gouged scars down the cheeks even onto the throat, then more scars across, the same scars Lee-Tan had cut into her son's face to make people fear and follow him. Anzeel slashed and cut and thrust at the stone, as if he wanted Torfinn to bleed. But it was Nyori who bled inside. For this boy who had said he could never be a scratcher, who said he could never make pictures like hers—he had done something she never would: had captured meanness on a tablet of stone.

Anzeel's hair fell down across his face as he finished. When his face swung upward, the hair flipped back from his eyes, which fixed on Nyori. Only a moment before he hadn't cared what she said. No. He had told her to shut up. Now the eyes stared into her with anxious, blue intensity.

"What?" he said. "What do you think?" She couldn't make her mouth open to answer him. He lifted the stone from his lap and dropped it in the dirt. "It's no good!"

The words blew out of him in a blast of breath. He glanced

away from her, out into a world of snowflakes that only swirled in the air without really falling. He sat still, even his chest was still, as if he no longer breathed. She had never told him his scratching was good. Because it never had been? Because she was jealous and unfair? Nyori felt the steady bleeding inside herself.

"It's ugly and awful," she said, "and wonderful."

He kept his face turned away, but the breathing came back. His shoulders heaved as he sucked in cold air and breathed it out in clouds. Now that she had heard it, she realized that was the word. Wonderful. She was also breathing quickly, almost in time with him.

"Remember Irta!" The voice came from behind them. She spun around to see Drogben staring at the picture of Torfinn. "Deep Earth is her womb, everything is born of it. Whatever we scratch on the walls, those things appear on the prairie above, on the tundra, in the forest..."

"This is not Deep Earth," Anzeel said.

"It's not on the walls!" Nyori yelled. "Torfinn won't appear."

Ruefully, Drogben shook his head.

"Scratcher Woman, I hope you're right."

17

Trapped in Deep Earth

Where rounded hills began to rise up ahead, the Blue Mountains floating above them on a raft of clouds, there Scratcher raised his arm and stopped the Horse Band in its march. By now the old man was so blind he could recognize only light and dark and familiar shapes. Yet with his head up, his face turning as if to search hillsides in the sun of afternoon, he seemed to see through his wrinkled ears.

"Ravens," he said. "I hear only ravens. Other birds stopped calling. No woodpeckers. No little birds."

Once he said it, everyone else heard the same. Nyori and Anzeel, Drogben and Kansi, stood at the head of the column with him. For most of a moon they had been on the march from the Shelter, returning heavy laden toward their summer home in Owl cave. They had planned to arrive long before nightfall, but this silence stopped them.

"Why don't birds sing?" someone said.

Just as Kansi with her keen eyes had first recognized the enemy hiding near Owl Cave, she was first this day with an answer.

"Ah! There, to the right beyond the trees!"

Nyori looked where Kansi pointed and saw a shape go out of sight behind greening branches. A moment passed before they saw more shapes skulking from tree to bush, from bush to boulder. Three or four Wolf-Kills were trailing them on that side.

Moving on, they soon saw one ahead, a single wolf mask that appeared above a rock and slid out of sight. When they reached that place, the man had vanished. Then two on the left. Scratcher saw none of it, but Kansi told him what was happening. Abruptly, he called another halt and stood in the trail, looking blindly at the ground.

"This is Torfinn. He knows our pathways. Knows when we come."

"Give me Anzeel and Rothgar," Drogben growled. "We'll run the jackals down."

Then, recalling that bright splash of blood on the snow, Nyori thought of the poor Cave-Brow who, alone, had been chased down and killed by a band of Wolves.

"No," Nyori said. "If we fight, we fight together."

She felt big, felt important when she said it—and wondered whether they would listen to Scratcher Woman Behind his blind eyes, old Scratcher seemed pleased.

"Good. All right, what? What now?"

Nyori was about speak when Anzeel broke in.

"They're off among the rocks. We're on the trail. We can move faster and leave this bunch behind. Once we get into Owl Cave, we have a better chance."

Troubled, the old man again turned his face to the ground. The nearly-bald skin of his crown shone in slanting sunlight.

"When we get ahead," he murmured, "they'll come up on the trail. They'll overtake us."

"Let's just try," Nyori said, "run for the cave."

She slid an arm around Anzeel, her hand pressing his narrow waist on the far side. As Scratcher had told them back at the Shelter, now they were man and woman, they were one. One person. She hugged Anzeel, shoulder to shoulder, hip to hip, and felt a rush of happiness when he hugged back. Drogben wasn't happy. Swinging gloomy eyes to the hills around, where Wolf-Kills seem to thicken moment by moment, he said:

"Someone may die today."

The strongest men and women took up took up a child to carry. Then the Horse Band stepped out. They would trot awhile, slow to a fast walk, then trot again. Burdened by bundles of tanned leather, their travel rations of dried meat, extra garments, packs filled with needles of bone, flint lance points, burins and scrapers and knives, they struggled forward. Far ahead, the Blue Mountains no longer floated amid clouds.

132

Now they stood rooted firmly in the earth. The trail wound among boulders, crossed creeks foaming with snowmelt, twisted through tree groves, rising always higher into the hills. Scratcher couldn't keep up. Panting, pumping his skinny arms and legs, he drifted back along the line toward the rear.

Anzeel and his woman, Nyori and her man, they drifted back with him. When Otti could no longer keep up, each took one of his hands. They half carried, half towed the child between them, Otti sometimes lifting his feet, crowing at the sun, delighted to see the earth speed backwards under him. Nyori knew she might soon begin to feel a child within her, a child to be Otti's niece or nephew. Though there was yet no sign, the signs could come any day. Anzeel glanced across at her.

"What are you grinning about?" he asked.

"Nothing!" she panted.

Above the hills, above the mountains with their shining glaciers, crisp clouds seemed to hang quite still against the blue of sky. Yet their shadows, spotting the land as far as she could see, swept with amazing swiftness across pale-green prairie, across black-green forest groves. One shadow came from behind, darkened the world so Nyori felt the cooling shade on her sweaty neck. Then it raced ahead. She turned her face up and let the reappearing sun blaze on it, just as Anzeel sang out beside her.

"It's a beautiful day!"

"Yes! And not the one to die in," she said. Now Anzeel smiled.

"We can't die. Since Scratcher taught us how, we've got to paint Empty Cave. We won't die!"

Such a surge of blood pounded in her veins that she almost fell. *She loved him.* They stumbled on carrying Otti between them, casting glances into each other's eyes. Those at the head of the fleeing Horse Band stopped at a narrow passage between a cliff on one side and tall boulders on the other. They waited for Anzeel and Nyori to come up, Otti sagging between. Drogben stood in the trail and pointed behind them.

"They're catching up," he warned. "Here we can ambush them."

Anzeel studied the rocks on both sides and said:

"Not here, Drogben. Here the Wolf-Kills will expect it."

Anzeel, the foster son, was telling Drogben what to do. Would

133

he respond with anger? No, he just shrugged and hurried forward on the trail. Farther along, with the narrow passage still in sight, Anzeel dragged them to a halt. A single boulder towered on one side. Full-leafed hazel shrubs grew thickly around its base, their drooping, worm-like yellow flowers already fading..

"Here," Anzeel said.

"Yes," Drogben barked. His big hand squeezed Anzeel's shoulder as he grinned down on the boy. "Smart!"

The oldest and youngest members of the Horse Band went slowly onward, Mayro leading Otti by the hand. They would wait just out of earshot down the trail. The strongest fighters, five men, three women, settled behind the boulder amid hazel branches. They found just enough cover to hide themselves. But, facing such odds, so many enemies, Nyori began to wonder what would happen.

"When the Wolf-Kills come," she said, "don't cast your lances. Just surprise them, then stand and threaten. Just prove that we could kill them."

Drogben smiled down on her.

"Soft!" he said. "So soft. All right, but we need one. One lance."

Preparing a surprise, the Horse fighters were surprised themselves at how quickly it developed. They were barely ready when seven—no, Nyori counted, nine—Wolf warriors appeared. They came warily through the narrow place, as Anzeel had predicted. Then they loped forward toward the hazel thicket ambush, wolf tails of their headdresses lifting behind them on the wind. Most carried short fighting spears, a few brandishing battle axes above their heads as they ran. They squinted into the sun hanging halfway down the sky.

Then a lance shot past the leader and lodged, quivering, in the trail ahead of him. They skidded to a halt, raising little clouds of dust, one of them falling down. They glanced wildly around, paniced eyes showing behind the wolf masks. Horse Band fighters rose from the thicket and stepped forward. Their lances were raised on throwers, ready to cast. The tallest Wolf, a man with a horse tail of blond hair to his waist, threw off his mask and stood open mouthed before them. In order to cool himself, he had folded back his tunic. His hairless chest, panting still from the chase, was bared to their blades.

"Weapons down!" Drogben growled at the Wolves.

Again Nyori was surprised—this time because the Wolf-Kills obeyed. They shed their lances, battle axes, even their flint knives when Drogben demanded it. All fell into dirt at their feet. Drogben pointed back down the trail.

"Go!"

They started slowly, looking behind them. The tall one flashed a twisted smile and flipped a hand up, as if waving goodbye. Then they ran. Drogben, Nyori and Anzeel and his mother, Kansi, stood boldly out on the trail, choosing a few of the weapons for themselves and breaking shafts of the rest. The Wolf-Kills tumbled back through the narrow cliff passage, one pausing to howl, hyena-like at the end, rising in maniac laughter. Hardly two breaths later, the same cry rang from a hill far to the right of the trail—an echo? Drogben took hold of Nyori's arm.

"Look."

A line of Wolf-Kills rose slowly above the hillcrest, a few wearing wolf masks, most bare headed under the sun. Even without sight, Scratcher sensed the danger, turning his face in that direction.

"How many?"

"Many!" Anzeel breathed.

"All those behind us," Scratcher said. "Now these ahead. Where are they coming from?" Then he answered his own question. "This is not the one Wolf Band. It's all Wolves together. Skuuhl called in the whole tribe for us." Quick breaths rattled in his throat, Scratcher sucking air as if every breath hurt. "I brought us to this," he said. "I led us back."

Kansi squeezed his wrinkled arm.

"We always come back. We always do. Scratcher, you saved us before."

Many times he had saved them, of course, but now he seemed shaken.

"What do we do?" he said, as if this time he didn't know. Nyori spoke up.

"Do what Anzeel said, run for the cave."

"Yes, run! Yes!"

Scratcher was so eager for her answer that Nyori felt sorry she'd given it. They ran. The fighters caught up with the rest of the band, again sweeping small children up for carrying, hurrying others along. Nyori began to see the Horse Band's packs and bundles thrown off along the trail. She threw off her own pack. Life was worth more than tanned leather, more than shell-decorated tunics. The line of Wolf-Kills went out of sight behind a hill, following them on that side. But the boldest among them in twos or threes rushed down toward the Horse column and—at extreme distance—cast their lances. None quite reached a target.

Anzeel ranged out on that side. With quick throws, he cast four Wolf-Kill lances back at one jeering group. When the fourth glanced off a boulder beside them, the jeering stopped. They turned and ran. That group would give away no more lances to a such a thrower. But it was Anzeel who came back bleeding from a little cut on his forehead.

. "Threw so hard, I fell down," he sighed, wincing as Nyori mopped blood from his cheeks and suddenly smiling lips. "Hit my head."

He had done it, Anzeel had driven that bunch away. It was Nyori who felt the pride. She pulled the load of leather from his shoulders and dropped it beside the trail.

"Come."

Nyori and Anzeel had worked their way back to lead the racing column when another line of Wolf-Kills rose on the flank of the leftward hill, only three at first, then a multitude—more warriors there than on the other side. The Horse Band rushed to get ahead, Nyori beginning to recall her band's great bison hunt, how they had chased the animals, how they drove the bison over the cliff. No cliff came before Owl Cave, she was glad for that. But it seemed they of the Horse Band also were being driven like fleeing animals.

Ahead of the rest, Nyori and Anzeel hurried knee deep in ferns through the meadow where so long ago he had lanced the little horse colt. They were nearly home. Pausing on a rise amid flowering thorn rose, Nyori saw the river mouth of the cave, black water boiling there. The troubled pool would be deep, hard to swim through. Better if they could push on around the hill to the dry entrance. She buried her face in a cluster of white thorn-rose, its crushed-raspberry sweetness aching in her chest. She thought how wonderful, how unusual, had been this passage of four seasons. With all its trials, this passage had been the best of her life. Her man stopping beside her, she caught a breath and said:

"Anzeel, we're back where we started last spring, and all of us are alive. None of us died."

His hand came out to touch her cheek, slid back to curve around her neck. His own neck shone with sweat, dirt ground into its creases. His eyes were darker now than the sky beyond his face.

"Yes," he said.

Otti came toward them up the trail, Mayro holding one of his hands, the other cheerfully waving at his sister. Then came Drogben, Scratcher, Rothgar, Riba, Kansi, Cheemee, Wanchuck and the others, laboring up the hill. They neither waved nor smiled. They panted with the effort, throwing fearful glances to the rear.

Behind them, the slope crawled with Wolf-Kills ranged in a ragged line. The ranks sagged back where warriors stumbled through trees or rocks, raced forward where the ground was grassy. Their battle signals—whistles, barks, little howls—rang on the air. Never had she seen so many men bristling with weapons.

Anzeel and Nyori waded into the water, starting to ford the little river to go around the hill. Others followed. Feeling icy water on their feet, the Horse Band cheered.. This was the river that came out of the hill. They had not reached the middle when a shower of lances erupted from a willow thicket on the far shore—so many that Rothgar's instinctive dodging caused him to dart in the way of one. He took it through the thigh, yanked it out and blindly hurled it back. Drogben helped him as they retreated to solid ground. Already here the earth was littered with fallen lances, studded with lances plunged upright in the soil. Surely the enemy had not been aiming to kill—otherwise no Horse man or woman would be standing now. Anzeel kept his own lance but picked up none of the Wolf weapons they'd thrown away.

"I don't know why," he said. "They don't throw to hit us, so I won't hit them."

This time it was the Horse Band that had been ambushed. The yellow-green tangle of willows on the far shore, which moments ago had moved so prettily on the breeze, trembled violently as Wolf-Kills marched through to the open river bank, another line equal to the one coming up the hill. But where was Torfinn?

Now the Horse Band dare not run around to the cave's dry

entrance. They couldn't escape uphill, because the battle line also curved above. They clustered in awed silence as Kansi described the situation to the old man. Between thumb and forefinger, he scritch-scritched his chin.

"What do we have," Scratcher mused, "that would bring out so many of them for so few of us? We left the hides behind. We left the unhafted flints. They've thrown away more lance points chasing us than they'll ever get from us. What do they want, our tunics? Our *trousers*?"

Nyori burned with impatience at his puzzlement.

"Scratcher, what do we *do?*"

His bony shoulders lifted in a shrug, then sagged.

"Who am I to say? I brought you to this."

Hearing him take the blame, Nyori felt her bones loosen in their sockets, sorrow flowing into her joints.

"What if it was my fault, Scratcher? I went to Deep Earth. I scratched pictures in Irta's womb. Now she's angry with us."

His moist eyes stared into her.

"No. Our Irta cannot be so bad."

Somehow, the old man had changed. When she tried to hug him, he fended her off.

"No! Nyori, you decide, you and your man."

Already Anzeel's eyes were searching for the answer. Nyori looked too. The Wolf-Kills across the river stood firm, but the ranks on the hillside behind them kept coming. The warriors chattered among themselves, raising little cries, as if to build courage for the charge. Her eyes turned to Anzeel.

"Swim into the cave?" she said.

"They'll be waiting there."

"Not these," she said, waving her hand from the approaching warriors to the waiting ones on the far river bank. "These, at least, we won't have to fight."

"Into the cave then!"

"I'll stay," Scratcher said, "slow them a little. Anyway, I can't swim."

"You shall!" Anzeel grabbed the old man's arm. "We all go!"

They waded in together, children beginning to wail as ice water rose from hips to chest to chin. Strong swimmers on the outside of the group, weak ones inside. With leather strips, with cords of braided tendon, they bound themselves in a tangle, the Horse Band of many people now become one, like Anzeel and Nyori, like a wetted rawhide knot that shrinks in the sun till it cannot be untied.

They were about to dive into Deep Earth, which before had been such a terror to women of the band. Nyori's eyes met those of Kansi, finding no fear in them. Deep Earth belonged to her now—as much to women as to men, for whatever that might be worth this day. When the rock above began to reach down toward their heads, Nyori shouted:

"Breathe! Everyone breathe! Make yourself dizzy, then hold the biggest breath."

As her eyes went under, she glanced back and saw Wolf-Kill lances spear the water behind them, trailing strings of bubbles to the rocky bottom, where they glanced away and rattled past beneath. She swam with both arms, kicked wildly, her belt helping tow the mass of them. Anzeel, Wanchuck, Kansi, Drogben and other strong swimmers towed beside her. Anzeel was tall enough now so that his feet soon found bottom. He walked with arms raised high, pushing the group ahead. Soon Wanchuck and even the wounded Rothgar did the same, powerfully battling the current. She saw Otti's face, air bubbling from his nose, his eyes asking a question of her in this gray twilight. When could they breathe? When?

Nyori wanted to see only blackness ahead, the utter cave darkness that would mean escape. It never quite came. This time—as water chilled her open eyes—the light changed from gray to brown, then to rosy pink like a dawning day. But this was no dawn. Desperate, they all groped upward, banging their heads on rock. They clawed forward and at last broke through, gasping, coughing, sucking air, the children screaming—some not able to scream.

Nyori's feet touched bottom. Her left hand caught the back of Otti's head, the right lifted his chin above the surface. Otti breathed, shuddering, his question answered at last. Anzeel held Scratcher's head up as the old man coughed, water gushing from his mouth. Swift hands cut the ties that held them all together, the one person of their band once more becoming many. Hairy heads bobbed thickly on the surface. It seemed they all had made it, all her people alive.

Instead of darkness around them, they found a rock-arched

ceiling ablaze with light, the air starred with torches, a leaping fire of driftwood at the far end of the gravel beach. Faintly, she heard the roar of rapids from distant depths of the cave. The walls gleamed wetly, giving back the light. Blinded, Nyori blinked and saw that for every torch holder, there were two or three warriors armed with lances and clubs. The air reeked of wood smoke and wet wolf pelts.

Her eyes searched for Torfinn in the brightness beside the fire. His voice roared out instead quite close, just to her right on the gravel beach.

"See the Hoppers! They don't hop now!"

Yet he was hopping, Torfinn was, gleefully dancing about. Sitting quietly near him on a driftwood log was the old man Nyori had seen before, wolf-masked, eagle-winged. An eagle-headed staff was planted in the gravel beside him. He extended a withered hand as if to stop Torfinn, who instantly began a pleading chant.

"Father Skuuhl, I did this. I gave you victory over these Irta-haters. See how once again they have brought women to Deep Earth. Irta wants their BLOOD!" This word he shouted, and the echo rang in the chamber. "Come, father, Irta wants blood NOW!"

Nyori did not believe in Irta. She knew she must pretend and still was surprised to hear her own muttering, "Irta, help me! Help me pretend!"

Her feet found the sloping gravel of the beach. She climbed toward shore, melted ice raining from her tunic as the cave air warmed her skin. A thick-chested warrior advanced with his kill spear leveled toward her chest. Then she found herself wrestling not with the Wolf-Kill but with Anzeel, who, lance in hand, boiled up from the water to defend her.

"Stop, Anzeel! Don't!"

Arms squeezing his heaving chest, she tried to calm him as another spear man closed in. Then a voice croaked out in the chamber.

"Don't touch her! Leave her be!"

It was Skuuhl. Leaning on his staff, he rose to his feet, the tattered brown wings of his costume flopping wide behind his shoulders. Surprised, Torfinn glanced across the flames at the Wolf-Kill chief. Nyori pried the lance from Anzeel's fingers.

"They'll kill you. Give it to me!"

Holding her man's hand, Nyori looked at Torfinn and went blind, angry tears flooding her eyes, melting all torchlight into one luminous pool. No, she did not believe, yet she screamed:

"Torfinn pretends to know Irta! But he knows only Lee-Tan's ambition, her desire to make her son the chief. Irta, our Mother, wants no blood!" She waited for the echo to die, then lowered her voice and spoke again. "*My* Mother Irta is better. Her world is not like that." She panted the words out. She started to say, "we make...we make," but—fearful of the warrior's spear point—changed the word.

"We *choose* our gods. Choose a bad god, you make your world horrible. Remember the day outside this cave? She made it beautiful. Beautiful." Nyori recalled what Kansi had said when she knelt at the Deep Earth Arch. Now she shouted it out. "Our Mother, our Mother Irta is *good*, she is *so* good!" Believing in Irta as she said it, then before the echoes died away, not believing.

Skuuhl didn't seem to hear. He stood like a long-dead tree, loose-barked and tottering. Abruptly, he plucked up his eagle-headed staff and swung it down to point straight at Nyori.

"YOU!" he barked. "I have been told it was you who made the picture of your Scratcher in the Womb Shrine. Of your Scratcher dancing. In coming here today, I saw it once more. Your Scratcher *dancing*. Dancing forever! Dreadful! Like a god!"

So dreadful, Nyori thought, that Skuuhl himself had recoiled from the picture. Thus had it halted the Wolf-Kill pursuit through the cave. Would he now kill her for stopping them? For making a god dance on the wall? Is that why all Wolf-Kills had gathered to drive them into this trap? If so, why hadn't they already killed the Horse People? She didn't understand. Yet she could not deny one truth, of which she was proud.

"YES, I made it!"

A huge sigh, a great, "Ahhhhhhhhhhhh...." rose from the crowd of Wolves. Their chattering echoed and re-echoed through the chamber. Many Wolf warriors, but not Torfinn, began to shuffle, muttering sing-song incantations. Nyori's own people shifted uneasily behind her at the water's edge. She felt Anzeel at her shoulder and moved his lance to her other hand, so he couldn't reach it.

"You!" Skuuhl shouted again at Nyori. "You will make a

picture of ME! Bigger. Bigger than the picture of your Scratcher. More awful. *More* like a god. To live FOREVER! Make my picture, and you will not die."

So that's why they'd been trapped like marmots in a hole! This amazed Nyori and seemed to stun Torfinn. He reached a pleading hand out toward the old man.

"No! No, Father Skuuhl!" he groaned. "I told you, *I* will make your picture. BIG. In the Womb Shrine. Make you like a god. Thus, you will live forever."

Skuuhl flapped a hand at him.

"I have seen your pictures. Not you for pictures. So, kill the rest of them, but leave her. If she makes me a god, she lives."

Kill the rest. At those words the fighting spears and lances of the Horse People came up. Anzeel reached around her body, grappling for the lance she'd taken.

"Give it back!" he yelled.

She stepped away from him, took one stride toward Skuuhl and jammed the butt of the lance into gravel at her feet. She jerked up the flap of her tunic and pressed the point to the little mound of her left breast, where their child might nurse if ever they were allowed to have one. Anzeel had chipped the flint so sharp it pierced her flesh there. Ah! That hurt! Blood ran out to flow down her belly onto the leather trousers. The stab wound was small, but a bleeder. Torfinn's Irta wanted blood. Nyori was offering it.

Skuuhl threw down his staff, feebly raising both hands palms out in a gesture of alarm. His eyes, ringed with puffy bluish flesh, blinked wildly.

"Skuuhl!" she yelled at him. "I will make your picture. Bigger than Scratcher's. More like a god. DREADFUL! To live forever, and in a cave much greater than this one. But if you kill even one of us, I die also. Now or later, you cannot stop me. Kill any of us and you kill me."

Already her wound throbbed with each racing heartbeat. She gritted her teeth against the pain. She felt Anzeel's hands grip her shoulders to hold her away from the lance. Still, with a thrust from her arms she could plunge it in. But that little cut hurt so. It *hurt*! With her people gathered behind her, Nyori stood trembling at the water's edge, wondering whether she could do it after all—whether she could endure the full, jagged bite of flint.

Then she noticed once again the sound of the river, the hollow roar of rapids from deep in the cave, even little wavelets rippling onto the gravel at her feet. Except for that, it was so quiet. The shuffling had stopped. She glanced up and saw that Skuuhl's hands, thrown wide before, had jerked in to clamp together over his mouth. He stared wide eyed at her. The rest of them stood rooted to the gravel, also staring as if in horror. They gaped at the widening dribbles of blood down the front of her garment. Nyori found this hard to believe—savage Wolf-Kill warriors shocked, like their leader, at the sight of blood.

18

Lead!

That night they slept, or tried to sleep, in the meadow outside the dry entrance of Owl Cave, so familiar yet now very different, a little band of Horse People amid a huge murmuring encampment of Wolf-Kills. This was like the storied Great River Conclaves of old, Horse People and Wolf People living together, at least for the moment, in something like peace. Though not the full Horse Tribe this time, just their own band surrounded by the whole tribe of Wolves. The night was moonless. Above them the black sky blazed with stars.

Wrapped in bison robes their captors had offered, Nyori and Anzeel lay side by side, face to face, near glowing coals of a fire.

"We didn't die," she whispered.

"No." His hand came out to touch her cheek. It felt warm against her skin.

"We're alive, Anzeel. All of us. Still."

"It wasn't the day to die." He stroked the cheek and drew his hand back. "What will happen tomorrow?" She didn't answer, because of course there was yet no answer. "Irta-love kills people," Anzeel said. "It *can* kill. But it saved us today. Because of your scratching, Irta-love saved us. I believe in *that* Irta, the one you spoke of in the cave."

"I know."

"And you don't."

"No."

"Why? *Why* not? After so much time has passed, is it only because she didn't save your mother?"

"Not just that. Because Irta let my mother die, I hated her. I don't *want* to hate her, Anzeel. I don't want to blame her. That's why I don't believe in her. But you can. I don't mind."

This didn't satisfy him, she realized, or her. They lay awhile looking into each other's eyes. After the long flight and fears of that terrible day, she thought they would lie forever awake. Then, abruptly, her eyes blinked open as dawn brightened the sunrise sky, pink near the horizon spreading slowly upward into blue above. A fiery twist of cloud hung level above a distant line of forest.

She sat up blinking. Around the earth-pallets of the Horse Band, someone had set down many bags and packs and bundles. Fumbling through the nearest, she saw these were Horse belongings, things they'd discarded as they fled along the trail, tanned leather, extra garments, a fat packet of dried bison flesh, even some unhafted flints. It seemed all had been returned to them.

Hungry, Nyori pawed the packet open and chewed a strip of meat. It was tough, with little taste, still better than nothing. The Wolf warriors moving about the camp had put aside their masks. Without them, they looked like men, just ordinary men, except their garments were shabbier than those of Horse People. Some carried dry branches to women re-kindling cookfires. Others moved through, hunched under the weight of what looked like butchered reindeer parts. All too often Nyori had seen Wolf warriors, but never before a Wolf woman. Mostly they, too, were a raggedy lot, their trousers worn to strips at the leg ends, tunics stained and tattered. The youngest children ran bare bottomed about the camp.

No one else among the Horse People was yet awake. They were still exhausted from that grueling chase. Anzeel slept with his mouth open, fine fur of the bison robe moving on his inward and outward breathing. With one hand she smoothed and flattened the fur so he wouldn't suck in loose hair.

"Is he your man?"

Nyori's eyes jerked up to see a Wolf, the very one with a blond horse tail hanging to his waist, a man as old as Drogben. She was slow answering, so slow a smile grew on his face—the same twisted smile he'd thrown back at them on the trail.

"Well," he said, "save the dried rations for when you have nothing better." He passed her a hefty leather pack, in which she saw two smaller leather bags along with much raw reindeer flesh, fat loins among the other cuts. A meal for everyone in her band. He said: "Get water from the creek. You can go that far." That far but no farther, she judged.

"Thank you," she said anyway. "Yes, he's my man."

"Oh, I thank *you*," he came back. "I stood helpless before your weapon. You didn't use it. Thank you, Scratcher Nyori. I am Sabol." He cast an assessing eye on the sleeping Anzeel. "He's young, but he knows the lance. I saw the one long throw. Still, it's good that he missed."

"He knows more than the lance," she said. "He too makes pictures."

"Hmmmm! Three scratchers in so small a band, one old and two young. Oh, you scared us," he said, "when we chased you through the cave last fall. You scared us with that scratching! Master Skuuhl ran away with the rest. Then, when he saw it later, the picture made him want to live forever, like your old Scratcher."

He shook his head and smiled again, as if the Wolf attack and Horse escape had all been a game. She would never understand Wolf warriors—or any warrior who could think it was no more than a game. Serious now, he squatted and peered into her face.

"Master Skuuhl told me you swore you would make his picture, make him a god, in a cave much greater than this one. Where is it, this great cave?"

"Toward sunrise sky from these mountains." She pointed. "Half a moon toward the Ice. We can show you."

"He's not well," Sabol said. "He's worse this morning, but he wants to leave today. Wants the picture before he dies."

His eyes were black black as the darkest heart of a cave, yet strangely amiable. She saw herself reflected in them. This emboldened Nyori.

"What will happen *after,* after I make the picture? What will happen to us?"

But he wasn't looking at her. His eyes had darted to something beyond her. She turned and saw it was Torfinn and his mother, Lee-Tan, standing by a cookfire half a lance cast distant. They stared back under lowered brows. She swung around to Sabol.

"*Tell me.* What will happen?"

"Not now," he murmured. "Later."

He jumped to his feet and was gone, marching vigorously, swinging this way and that to round a cookfire or a cluster of chatting women folk. So, even here in Torfinn's home tribe, even with his father, people spoke warily in his presence. Nyori rewrapped her strip of dried meat. She would wait for something better. Anzeel was awakening when two women approached, the young one carrying firewood, the older one a blazing brand. He was barely on his feet when the elder grasped his hand, folding it around the base of the torch.

"Your people must cook and eat," she croaked. She pointed to the sky overhead. "At sun-peak we start on the trail."

The other knelt, building a pile of criss-crossed twigs over the dead coals of last night's fire, then reaching for the brand Anzeel held. When the twigs caught, she lay larger branches on, the flames licking up, a thread of smoke slanting out with the breeze across the encampment. The younger woman looked up sharply at Anzeel and said:

"You let *her* go to Deep Earth?"

It seemed a hostile question. How would he answer? Nyori wondered.

"*Let* her?" he said. "I can't *stop* her. This time a year past, she swam against the river into Deep Earth. Didn't ask anybody. Just swam in. Now we go in together. All in our band, men and women, we all go there."

Though he had opposed Nyori through some of that struggle, he said this not as if in shame, but proudly. She felt a rush of warmth for him. The younger woman rose to stand beside the fire she'd kindled. She was blond like Sabol and freckled under her eyes, but with hair hacked off short, barely covering her ears. She looked keenly into Nyori, her face flushing even as she asked the question.

"Are you old enough to bleed?"

More about blood, Nyori thought, though of course a different kind.

"Yes!" she said, surprised that, like Anzeel, she felt pride in answering the woman's question.

"What must you do then, when you bleed?"

Nyori shrugged.

"I braid a rope of soft grasses, twist it into a pad to cover. Then go on."

"Go on? Just go *on*? Don't you have to stay in the unclean place?"

What was she was talking about?

"No."

To her daughter, the old woman said: "I told you. Didn't I?"

Ah! *Women with their blood!* Their dirty blood. Here it was again, Torfinn's old cry, the echo ringing still. The young one's face flushed an even deeper pink, her breath coming quickly.

"I am Agah," she said. "This is my mother, Nema."

The mother's face was long past blushing, browned from sun, darkly wrinkled. Her tunic was torn a little at the neck, grease spattered on the sleeves, the garment of a fire-tender, of one who grills meat. The constant wood smoke must have coarsened her voice.

"Agah can't believe it was ever different," she growled. "She wasn't born when the fighting started at that Great River Conclave. Nor were you, Scratcher Nyori. I remember it. Master Skuuhl remembers. Your old Scratcher too. I knew him then. Then we were friends."

Impatient, the daughter broke in, her hot eyes fixed on Nyori.

"What *else* can your women do?"

"Agah, give off!" The mother paused, glancing about her, as if gauging who in the encampment might hear. Lowering her voice, she added: "Their women can do much, Agah. Horse People took a different path. I told you, before that Conclave our women did anything they could manage. We hunted! Yes, hunted with the men, or even by ourselves! Snow hares! Cook one on a slow fire, snow hare is tasty, better than reindeer." She stared into Nyori's eyes, as if expecting a challenge on this point. Then she looked at the fire. "That one Great River Conclave, that's when the shuffling took over. *Shuffling!* Then came *Wolf* Irta! After that came *Blood* Irta. Last fall Lee-Tan brought her son back to us. Ooooo!" she groaned. "If he becomes chief..."

She trailed off as a Wolf warrior approached dragging a rolled sheaf of leather, probably the makings of a shelter. Agah spoke out formally as he passed behind.

"You need to wake others of your band. Get the meal started, because we march at sun-peak." She pointed to the sky, as her mother had before. With the warrior out of earshot, Anzeel asked:

"Are they all against you, all the men?"

"No!" Agah breathed. "Not all men against. Not all women for us, but most are."

"Sabol," Nyori said. "He brought this meat. How is he?"

"My younger brother," Nema explained. "He's with us." Then, as another warrior passed close by, she announced: "I know many cures. Where you stabbed yourself, how is it? Let me see."

Now it had been mentioned, Nyori wondered herself. She drew up her tunic, embarrassed to see her belly smeared with dried blood, her trousers streaked ochre-brown with it. There had been no time to wash. The cut below her nipple, only the breadth of a thumbnail but deep, had clotted like a scab with granules of blood.

"Looks all right," Nema said, "right as a stab wound can look." She smiled when her eyes came up to meet Nyori's. "You frightened them with this. You frightened Skuuhl. He wants you to make his picture. Men are all talking about it this morning. "

As Nema moved away, Agah suddenly stepped forward and dropped to one knee. She extended her hand to the wound, lay two fingers just under it and looked pleadingly up at Nyori.

"We heard about what you said of Mother Irta Of our *good* Mother Irta. Help us! Help us, Scratcher Woman!"

Help them? How could she help them, her captors, through a god in whom she did not believe? Nema grabbed her daughter's shoulders and dragged the woman back to her feet, hissing:

"Stop! Agah, stop! You'll spoil it!" Nema pulled her away, walking backwards and grinning as if nothing had happened. Then they turned and moved off through the camp. By now the flames had built a small bed of coals, the beginnings of a cookfire. Anzeel's blue eyes swung up to Nyori's.

"Spoil *it*, " he said. "What *it*? What's Agah going to spoil?"

"Something," Nyori replied, "but what?"

Around them in the meadow, other Horse People were awakening, crawling up to stand, yawning and stretching. Drogben bent over Kansi, gently patting her cheek, pulling at one of her arms to rouse her. Not long after, Nyori and Kansi flaked fresh edges on their flint knives and sliced the reindeer flesh into strips. The others gathered. Soon meat hung on many sticks slanting out over the coals. In the small bags they found dried berries, also acorn kernels, boiled to remove the bitterness. The band clustered at the fire, chewing hungrily. The berries were deliciously sour, spicing the richness of broiled reindeer loin. Grease shining on his fingers and chin, Drogben looked around the circle of them.

"Horse People, we, gorging like Wolves!"

His was the first Horse smile she'd seen since the day before, since that awful chase and their capture. During the meal Anzeel told everyone of the coming march to faraway Empty Cave. There were a few groans, but most were pleased simply to have lived through the night and have the journey before them. Scratcher ate only a few bites, still lying on his robe. He couldn't get up. Yesterday's pursuit, the frigid swim into the cave, had injured him somehow.

"It's my time," he sighed. "You got to leave me and go on." Repeating what he'd often said before when he fell ill. Cheemee and Rothgar cut alder saplings, binding the trunks with rawhide to make a litter for him. This they padded with a thick-furred cave bear skin before lifting the old man onto it. "All this trouble!" he fussed.

With her hunger sated, Nyori began even to *feel* the stickiness of dried blood on her belly. She picked her way down a stony slope to the creek at meadow's edge. Anzeel followed, carrying their packs. Behind a screen of thorn rose, she shrugged herself out of her dirty tunic and shed her trousers, as did Anzeel. She kicked off her sandals and waded in, gasping as she ducked under icy water and rose, splashing her front. The blood on her skin softened and washed off in pinkish streams, leaving just the grainy line of the wound under her nipple.

By now the sun had climbed well up the sky, shining warm on her front. They stood smiling at each other's bodies, all this pale skin where sun seldom touched. It pleased her that Anzeel was so tall, so slim yet strong. In her pack she found her spare trousers, only a little dirty. She pulled them on and reached for the tunic she'd just thrown off to bathe. Though soiled, it was at least free of blood.

"Wait," Anzeel called. From his pack he drew out the shell-decorated tunic she had long ago returned to him. Lifting it by the shoulders, spreading it with his two hands, he laid it against her bare upper body.

"No," she protested. "It's yours."

"It's our best. Today you must have it, Scratcher Woman."

Well, it *was* nice, a garment finely stitched by Anzeel's mother, of red deer hide softly tanned, scraped thin and supple, chewed and soaked and washed so many times it had bleached nearly white. Nyori herself had sewn on the swirling decoration of pink shells. She folded and packed her dirty garments. Then, wearing the fresh tunic, she walked beside Anzeel back up the path. Already Wolf warriors were lining up for the march, forming a long column, their women drifting to the rear laden with bundles. Scratcher lay amid the Horse People, looking weary but at least comfortable on the bear skin. As she approached, his grin shone up. Somehow, through the clouds obscuring his vision, he noticed her fresh garment.

"Ho!" he grunted. "See Scratcher Woman. How comely!"

So they did, everyone looked at her. Sometimes people spoke of buxom Riba in such words—but never of Nyori. Her face burned under their gaze. Then she saw Sabol hurrying through the crowd toward them. Arriving, he swung one arm back toward the lengthening column, speaking breathlessly, urgently.

"Torfinn and his men want Horse People at the rear, with the women. He'll want to fight us about it, but you're going to the front with Master Skuuhl. All the Horse, all of you must be up front, where you can lead."

"Us lead?" Nyori said. "Why?"

He dropped down onto one knee near Scratcher and lowered his gaze. For an instant she dreaded he would pray to her, as Agah had earlier. No. His glance told her he only wanted to speak more privately. She dropped down with him, as did Anzeel. The three heads clustered close above old Scratcher's face.

"You must help us, Scratcher Nyori," he said. "We're sick of Torfinn and Lee-Tan's Irta-love. We're sick of Blood-Irta—this stupid clash between Shufflers and Hoppers. Look around. Look at us. We fight so much, fight even each other, we don't have energy to make proper garments. We've forgotten how. We want to bring back the old days, what I remember from when I was boy.   We can start with your little band, later try to bring the whole Horse Tribe in. Horse Tribe and Wolf Tribe together."

He seemed a decent man, unbelievable for a Wolf. Still, now that this question had arisen, she couldn't get out of her mind the blood trail she'd seen so long ago on the snow, that hairy body being dragged by its feet.

"Horse and Wolf together, that would be fine," she said. "But what about Cave-Brows?   Last spring, in the last snow, I saw your Wolves chase a man down. They slaughtered him. It was terrible."

Sabol's two hands came together in a sharp slap against both sides of his head. He stared at the grass, taking long breaths. He held one for a moment and then sighed it out.

"It happened!   I wasn't there, couldn't stop it if I had been. There's a chance we can change that. With your help, we can change everything."

His face lifted to her now, eyes shining, as if he expected wonders of her.

"What do you *want*?" she cried. "What can *I* do about it?"

"BE OUR SCRATCHER!" he boomed.   Many faces in the crowd swung around to them. He lowered his voice. "Your Mother Irta is *so* good. Tell us what *your* Irta wants."

Often she had lied about this. Why not now?   But for some reason she spoke the truth.

"Sabol, I don't believe in Irta. My man does."

"I do, yes," Anzeel agreed. "I believe."

"Believe or not," Sabol said. "Both of you, *help* us. This is the time. If ever Wolf and Horse can come together again, this is the day."

"All right," Anzeel said. She only shrugged, but it was enough.

"Good!" Sabol grunted.. He jumped to his feet and pulled Nyori up, measuring her with his eyes, as if seeing her for the first time. "That's grand," he said, "your tunic." Again, Nyori felt blood run hot in the skin of her face.

"Anzeel's mother sewed it."

"It's perfect for today. We Wolves, we no longer make such handsome garments."

He asked Anzeel to stand beside him, hip against hip. Sabol

152

laced his fingers together, both his hands forming a cup, which he lowered toward her feet. "Step here."

She did and felt herself soar upward until she perched on two thick shoulders, Sabol's right, Anzeel's left. It was shaky for a moment, until each of the men passed an arm across the other's back, Wolf and Horse hugging each other side to side. With her high perch steadied, she gazed out over the crowd.

The Wolf column extended far uphill, leftward from the cave mouth, and far to the right, down the hill toward sunrise sky, a multitude of people tying bundles, lifting them to their backs, readying themselves for the march. The sun had almost reached its peak.

"Anzeel," Sabol said, "step together." They lurched forward, Nyori bracing herself with her hands on their heads. She glanced back at the Horse Band.

"We go!" she called.

Drogben and Rothgar lifted the front shafts of Scratcher's litter and fell in behind, letting the rear drag to scrape two ruts in the turf. Laden with their packs and bundles, the others followed. As Sabol had promised, he did not steer them toward the back of the column. They moved to the right, down the hill toward the front. From her high vantage, Nyori saw every face in the crowd turn to them, actually, to *her*, with eager eyes. As she approached the first group, the chattering subsided. Several women fell to their knees, throwing hands up prayerfully, as Agah had done.

After the great bison hunt, when—still a child—she first became Scratcher Woman, such homage had pleased her, made her feel powerful. Now it only caused an uneasy clenching in her gut. Still, she smiled and waved to the praying women. Instantly, a murmur rose from the crowd and a thicket of arms flew up to wave back at her, a moving flurry of hands that followed them as they moved.

Marching alongside the Wolf column, the Horse were approaching the front when a dozen masked Wolves stepped into the trail ahead. They carried no baggage, only war clubs and short kill spears.

"To the back!" Torfinn's voice spoke from behind one mask. "Father Skuuhl wants Horses to the back. Horse women behind the men. Irta demands it!." His hand shot out to point at Nyori. "You!   False Scratcher! Go!"

Nyori thought Sabol might now speak up, but he said nothing—just stood with Anzeel rock solid under her. For as long as she could remember, Torfinn had been against her—against every woman of the Horse Band except his own mother. Why? She didn't know but felt a red rage begin to burn behind her eyes.

"Never!" she bellowed, noting that at the single word, Torfinn's Wolves jerked backward one step. "Our Irta is good. She's good to men. She's good to women. Torfinn, move out of our way. Move!"

"Move!" Drogben bellowed from behind her—Drogben, the Horse who so long ago had pinched Torfinn's nose. Someone else repeated the word, "Move!" one repetition giving birth to another, spreading back through the crowd and then multiplying in a rumbling chant.

"Move! Move!" Impatient to start the journey, people back there were marching in place. When she waved to them, the thicket of hands sprouted up again to wave back.

"Move! Move! Move!"

Somehow Torfinn's Wolves held their ground. From below her, Anzeel sang out threateningly.

"Be-WARE the Mysteries!"

Yes! she thought. Mimicking Scratcher, Nyori threw both her hands up toward the sun, wiggling fingers as Scratcher did to suck spirits from the air—nonsense spirits that almost never worked. Still...

"Myster-EEEEES!" she screeched.

Flinching backwards at this, Torfinn's warriors began to thin on the trail ahead. Their masks came off. They melted into the column, no longer warriors of any kind—just shabbily-costumed male Wolves like all the others. Torfinn himself remained masked, moving only slightly off the path.

"Go!" Sabol said. He and Anzeel stepped out. Once again Nyori heard the reassuring scritch of the old man's litter behind them as the shafts scraped over rocky ground. Once again she saw Wolf faces, now men in the column, grinning up at her. But below the wolf mask, Torfinn frowned at Nyori, the point of his kill-spear following her as she passed.

They rounded a turn in the trail and reached the front, where—to Nyori's surprise—she saw Skuuhl himself stretched out on a litter much like old Scratcher's. Two Wolves held the shafts at the front, and more stood around him. His head lifted as he looked back toward the approaching Horse Band.

"Ha!" he yelled. "Is that Scratcher Suud on the litter? Well, haul him up here! Let me see." Drogben and Rothgar dragged Scratcher forward until the two were parked side by side. Skuuhl's mouth pursed like a dried plum, then stretched wide in a grin. "Look at you, Suud! You're worse off than I am! Got to be hauled around on a pile of sticks. Ha!"

The two old men lay grinning across at each other—taking what seemed to Nyori an insane pleasure in the meeting, since only yesterday Skuuhl had condemned Scratcher and the rest to death.

"Worse off, maybe," Scratcher replied, "but only because your Wolves ran our legs off, made us swim into that cave."

"Ha! In the old days you wouldn't make such excuses. Didn't we run then! Remember that last hunt for bulls on the steppe? You were way out front. Oh, you were a runner. You turned them into the trap, that little dead-end draw! Most meat we ever took in a day. Good bull meat! Don't you remember?"

"Sure I remember! " Scratcher boomed indignantly. "Eyes are bad, legs are bad—not the memory, not yet."

Skuuhl's eyes jumped confusedly from Scratcher to Nyori, still on her high perch, then swung back to the column stretching far to the rear. He seemed uneasy at the sight of this crowd.

"You know," Skuuhl said, "mine isn't so good anymore. The memory. Old stuff, I remember that." His eyes looked up to a sky milky just at the zenith with high feathery clouds. He inclined his head toward Scratcher and whispered. "Suud, what are we doing here? Why are all the people out? Looks like they're packed up to move."

"We're on the trail, going out to make your picture," Scratcher told him. "In Empty Cave. It's a good ways yet."

"Ah! Yes!" His eyes searched among those around him till they found Sabol. "Well, who will make my picture?"

"Here she is, Master Skuuhl." Sabol's hands came up to catch Nyori at the waist, lift her free of the two shoulders and bounce her down to earth. "This is Scratcher Woman. Scratcher Nyori. Remember, you saw the picture she made of Suud in the Womb Shrine."

Skuuhl's bleary eyes blinked at her.

"Oh! You're the one. Well. A woman Scratcher! Isn't that amazing." He looked again to Sabol. "I see we've got all the whole tribe out on the trail, just waiting back there. Should we be moving?"

"It's time, Master Skuuhl. Scratcher Nyori and her Horse People will lead. They'll lead us to the great cave."

"All right, that's fine. But I want Suud to stay here by me. We might talk a little as we go. About the old stuff, because I remember that."

"Old stuff!" Scratcher snorted. "How you split the water skin, spilled out all the drinking water. That day we got roasted by the sun like steak on a stick. We nearly died of thirst!"

"Now, now, did I bring up the stupid things you did? Just let that slip. Let it slip," he said, yawning. "We'll talk, but if you don't mind, Suud, as we go along I just might have a little nap."

"Nap!" Scratcher said. It seemed the word itself, potent as a brew of boiled herbs, made him drowsy. He yawned too. "Good idea. Nowadays I don't sleep much nights."

Leaving Scratcher behind with Drogben and Rothgar, the rest of the Horse Band pushed forward to lead. They followed a trail that wound down along the creek in which Nyori and Anzeel had bathed. Still milky at the zenith, the sky ahead was clear, its blue deepening as the afternoon wore on and their shadows stretched longer on the earth ahead. They could see far across the Land, hill on forested hill going away to a grassy plain in the distance. Making good time, they might reach the plain before nightfall to camp. She and Anzeel had walked quietly beside one another for awhile when he said:

"Isn't it strange? What Skuuhl could remember back there, all of it happened before that Great River Conclave. Before the fighting started."

Strange, yes, she thought, but not surprising.

"*Wolf*-Irta and *Blood*-Irta, he's forgotten that," Nyori said. "All the people they killed. All the terrible things he did. For him it's better that he can't remember."

Angling to the right, the trail went down a slope to the creek, where the current foamed between rough stones of a ford. Anzeel and Nyori helped his bearers haul Skuuhl across, then went back for

156

Scratcher. Somehow the old man had managed to nap even through this journey. With Drogben and Rothgar in front, she and Anzeel at the rear, they carried his litter across, Nyori's right foot skidding off on a stone, wetting that sandal. As they set him down on the other side, Scratcher's eyes opened. He smiled up at them. Then the eyes closed as once more he drifted off.

"From here we handle him," Drogben told them. "Go on ahead. Lead!"

Passing Skuuhl—also napping on his litter—Anzeel and Nyori again worked their way to the front, actually moving too fast, as they later noticed. The trail turned up onto a knoll, rocky but starred with red poppies, where they waited for the others to catch up. Behind them the Blue Mountains rose, their glaciers shadowed now as the sun slid farther down the sky. Stretching back into the foothills, the column of marchers came on, men and women and children, the whole Wolf Tribe and their own little Horse Band, all these people snaking toward them down the hill. Yes, and Torfinn also, Nyori thought, he was among them, still bearing all his grudges. As if reading her thoughts, Anzeel said:

"We're not finished with Torfinn. After this, he'll hate us more than ever."

"What will happen?" she said. "What will we do?"

"I don't know." Anzeel shrugged. "Something."

Behind them, the party with Skuuhl and Scratcher had reached the base of the rocky knoll and started up the shallow slope. *Lead!* Drogben had commanded, as if that were easy. Well, if not leading, at least she and Anzeel were ahead of the rest.

. "When we grow old," she told him, "we won't be like Skuuhl. We won't need to forget. We'll be like Scratcher. We'll remember good things."

"If we do good things, that's what we'll remember," he said.

"We will!" she insisted. "We'll do good things."

"I hope so. It's not easy."

For no real reason, she socked him on the left shoulder. He curled his right hand protectively over the spot, his blue eyes shining indignantly down on her.

"Hey!"

She took his other hand in her own and began pulling him along the trail.

"Come on."

That faraway grassy plain, it was not so far now. She could see where their creek met another as the ground leveled, forming a stream surely deep enough for salmon. This was the season for them too. Nyori decided they could easily reach the plain by nightfall and maybe even enjoy red-meat salmon for supper.

THE LEGACY

After nearly one hundred fifty centuries of Paleolithic art, one person or a few dared make real human portraits in La Marche rock shelter. Nothing quite like that had ever happened before. New things happened at Trois Freres cave, listed by the Abbe Breuil among his Six Giants of Paleolithic Art.

One work there still lies like a muddy jewel in the dark setting of a circular chamber. After its discovery in 1912, members of the Begouen family often led visitors on that 1,500-yard walk through the cave to see it. Seventy years ago one guest, German prehistorian Herbert Kuhn, was charmed by the guide's trick of waiting till the last instant, then illuminating the chamber. Of that moment, Kuhn wrote:

"We could not suppress a cry. The Bison Sculptures. Each beast is about two feet long as we see it by the flickering light of our lamps. These sculptures are no primitive carvings, they are works of surprising plastic beauty, filled with an astounding force of expression and rich with indwelling life."

The artist, of course, is long dead. But next month, next year, next century and beyond, a lucky few will make that subterranean journey to the gem of art which, after 15,000 years, could still call forth such a cry.

Enjoying that legacy...

Many months after their 1912 discovery, the maturing Begouen brothers with handsomely-costumed family, friends and archaeologists returned to the river Volp and the cave in a far better boat. They are among the first of thousands who would visit Trois Freres and its sister caves over the next century.

ACKNOWLEDGEMENTS

It's unusual for a novelist to acknowledge help with plain facts, but I am indebted to the whole great tribe of archaeologists, who struggle to discover the past lives from whence we humans come.

These include J. Mett Shippee, a field archaeologist nearly 50 years for the Smithsonian Institution and the University of Missouri. As a reporter for the Kansas City Star in the 1960s, I accompanied Mett on field trips to write of archaeological sites revealing the lives of ancient Native Americans, some from the archaic period 7,000 years ago. One brief life also encountered was that of an Indian baby tenderly buried about 1,000 A.D. and discovered by Mett in the dry earth of Arnold Research Cave near Fulton, Mo. Another was that of Mattie Alkire, born on Christmas day, 1863, during the American Civil War, who died the following May and was buried just as tenderly not a mile from the Indian baby.

I am indebted to those who first detailed the art treasures of Le Trois Freres and other nearby caverns of the Volp river, Abbe Henri Breuil, Count Henri Begouen and his three bold sons, Count Robert Begouen and all the family members who then and to this day preserve the caverns and their art.

Concerning the many human images discovered at La Marche, I particularly honor the work of the French archaeologist Leon Pales and his associate, Marie Tassin de Saint Pereuse.

I am indebted to Jean Clottes for his many literary books on archaeology, Evan Hadingham for his *Secrets of the Ice Age,* Herbert Kuhn for *On the Track of Prehistoric Man*, Andre Leroi-Gourhan for *The Dawn of European Art*, Andrew Marshack for *Roots of Civilization*, John E. Pfeiffer for *The Creative Explosion*, Mario Ruspoli for *Cave of Lascaux—The Final Photographs*, Ann Sieveking for *The Cave Artists* and Randall White for *Dark Caves, Bright Visions*.

Sources

Photo, 1912, of Begouen family members and archaeologists outside the Volp river cavern is courtesy of the Smithsonian Institution and Count Robert Begouen, grandson of the caverns' discoverer and present curator of the Caverns of the Volp Association.

All prehistoric images from the Volp river caverns, Trois Freres and Tuc d'Audobert, are courtesy of Count Robert Begouen, curator of the Caverns of the Volp Association.   Most of the engraved images are tracings made by the Abbe Henri Breuil in the early years of the 20th Century. Only one, of the Little Colt on page 21, is a photo of the actual image as scratched on the cave wall. The photo of the clay bisons is by J. Vertut.

All images from La Marche Cave were recreated for publication by Elise Ray, Graphic Artist, based on the engraved stone plaquettes themselves and the original deciphering by Leon Pales and his associate, Marie Tassin de Saint Pereuse

46.   Sculpture of bison spear thrower, courtesy of Musée d'Archéologie Nationale , Château de Saint-Germain-en-Laye, France. Being portable art, it was found in La Madelaine cave, from the same era as the art in Trois Freres.

119.   Painting of Aurochs or "bull," from Lascaux cavern courtesy of the Association Lascaux.

ABOUT THE AUTHOR

Charles Hammer was born in 1934 in Tulsa, Oklahoma. He earned spending money first by caddying for golfers, later working his way through the University of Tulsa. After U. S. Army service in Europe, he joined the Kansas City Star and did much of their reporting on the American Civil Rights Movement, 1958-1972. Later he taught journalism at the University of Missouri-Kansas City. He is co-author of *Unsportsmanlike Conduct*, a history of collegiate sports, two youth novels for Farrar, Straus and Giroux, a novel about elders, *Members of the Bored*, and a Civil War novel: *Emancipating---Black Soldiers (and a Peckerwood white boy) Free the Slaves*.

www.ingramcontent.com/pod-product-compliance
Lightning Source LLC
Chambersburg PA
CBHW060820120626
46557CB00001B/301